"*Kevin Kramer Starts on Monday* c
causes you to howl with laughte
sharply exposed horrors cut into you.
stories capture the absurdities of the 21st century corporate workplace in which white-collar millennials find their inboxes always brimming with new incentives for betrayal and self-betrayal. Neither the powerless nor the powerful outrun their demons in these brilliantly funny and bruising tales of American 'enterprise.'"

KEVIN McILVOY,
AUTHOR OF *THE COMPLETE HISTORY OF NEW MEXICO*

"Evoking Mike Judge, George Saunders, and Cate Dicharry in capturing the humor and dark panic in today's workplace, Graber's cast of corporate charlatans, doomed dreamers, and deluded strivers are brilliant and wholly original."

J. RYAN STRADAL,
AUTHOR OF *KITCHENS OF THE GREAT MIDWEST*

"Debbie Graber's stories are crisp, sardonic, and funny—as antic and acerbic as they are intelligent and alert. A sly and incisive observer of human nature, Debbie Graber will win you over with this delightful debut."

SARA LEVINE,
AUTHOR OF *TREASURE ISLAND!!!*

"*Kevin Kramer Starts on Monday* skewers that place where so many of us spend our days and about which we spend the other hours of our lives complaining: the modern workplace. In this bitingly funny, precisely crafted collection, Debbie Graber takes on office excess: happy hours, overtime, trysts, and petty grievances. In doing so, she questions our societal notions of success and failure and invites us to laugh at our bosses and coworkers and, perhaps most of all, ourselves—knowing that if we don't laugh, we just might cry. *Kevin Kramer Starts on Monday* is satire at its most incisive."

LORI OSTLUND,
AUTHOR OF *AFTER THE PARADE*

The Unnamed Press
P.O. Box 411272
Los Angeles, CA 90041

Published in North America by The Unnamed Press.

1 3 5 7 9 10 8 6 4 2

ISBN: 978-1-939419-84-2

Library of Congress Control Number: 2016936262

This book is distributed by Publishers Group West

Designed & typeset by Jaya Nicely

Kevin Kramer Starts on Monday

Debbie Graber

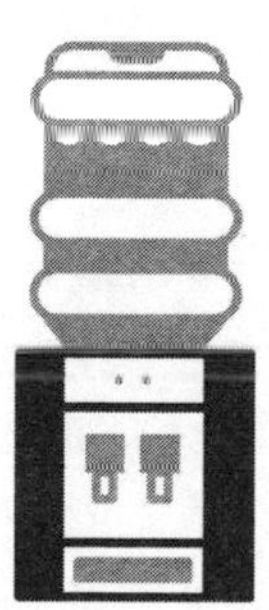

Contents

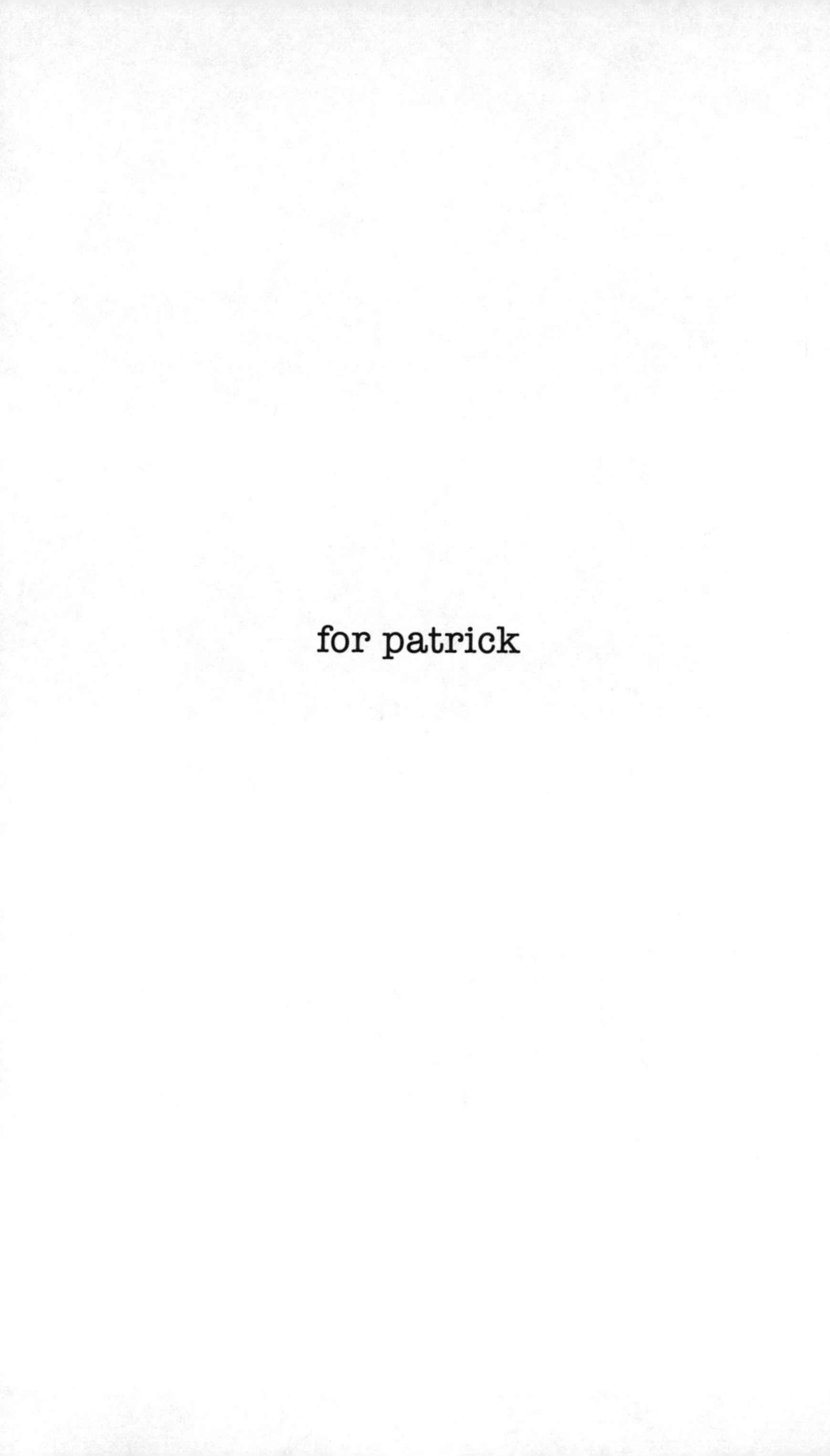

for patrick

Gregg Fisher's Pontiac Vibe

SOMEONE SAID THAT GREGG FISHER'S PONTIAC Vibe was the filthiest car they had ever seen.

Someone else said they noticed Gregg Fisher's Pontiac Vibe in the employee parking lot during a rainstorm, and that rivers of filth flowed down the car's roof. The filth created fluid designs on the hood and hatchback, designs that resembled spiderwebs, or paint drizzles like a Jackson Pollock painting. That person had recently seen the Pollock exhibit at LACMA.

Someone said the water designs on the hood of Gregg Fisher's Pontiac Vibe, when pictured out of context, could be considered beautiful. Someone else said that in context, the water designs were just putrid rivulets streaming down the roof of Gregg Fisher's Pontiac Vibe, so no one should ever think of them as artistic. Most people agreed.

No one can remember the last time that Gregg Fisher's car looked clean. Someone remembered that Gregg Fisher used to have a different car, a Plymouth Sundance or a Chrysler K-Car, they couldn't remember which. Someone else remembered that Gregg Fisher drove that car around the parking lot for years, until it started to emit thick, smelly smoke from the tailpipe. No one remembered who complained about the smelly smoke coming out of Gregg Fisher's tailpipe to HR, but shortly after, Gregg Fisher showed up to work driving the Pontiac Vibe.

No one could remember if the Pontiac Vibe had ever been new. Everyone agreed that it was impossible that anyone except for Gregg Fisher had ever been inside his Pontiac Vibe to smell "new car smell" or not. Whether Gregg Fisher bought his Pontiac Vibe new or used was debatable, and no one would ever ask Gregg Fisher about it. Most people refused to speak to Gregg Fisher out of principle.

No one can remember the last time Gregg Fisher cut his ponytail. Someone thought that it might have been in 1998, just after he started working at the company. Others swore that he's never been without his ponytail, that Gregg Fisher's ponytail is as much his trademark as is his Pontiac Vibe.

Gregg Fisher's ponytail is rough like a horse's tail. It is sprinkled with frizzled gray hairs. Someone remembered that Gregg Fisher's ponytail used to be thicker, but that, as the years passed, it had become scrawny. Someone else remarked that Gregg Fisher probably had to start using smaller scrunchies to get his thinning hair into a ponytail at all, but that Gregg Fisher would never shell out two dollars for a new set of scrunchies. Everyone agreed on that. No one looked too closely at Gregg Fisher's ponytail anyways. It grossed people out.

Another Gregg Fisher trademark was his commuter mug. Gregg Fisher brought his commuter mug to work with him every day. Someone once had the misfortune of sitting next to Gregg Fisher during a morning shareholder meeting, and witnessed the commuter mug up close and personal. This person was able to inspect the encrusted ancient stains of various colors along the sides of the mug, and the brackish buildup of muck around the part of the mug where Gregg Fisher put his hairy lip and slurped.

No one wanted to contemplate what kind of concoction Gregg Fisher was drinking out of his commuter mug, but out of a horrified curiosity, people offered suggestions. Someone mentioned aloe vera syrup. Someone else thought it was the leftover dregs of coffee from the coffeepot in the employee break room. Someone else thought it was animal blood, but no one believed that.

No one would ever choose to sit near Gregg Fisher in a morning meeting for fear of having to come into contact with the mug. Someone coined the phrase "typhoid mug" behind Gregg Fisher's back as a joke, but some people didn't find it funny. Some people were afraid of catching something if they sat too close to Gregg Fisher and his mug. Someone else said that merely breathing in the same general vicinity as Gregg Fisher, even without his mug, could make one's immune system weaker and cause medical issues. Someone else said that a software analyst's baby girl was born with not one, but two extra toes, and that Gregg Fisher must have had something to do with it.

Someone at the company was seriously afraid that Gregg Fisher was a carrier of the Black Death, and wrote an anonymous note to HR. But someone else said that no one in HR would be able to do anything, because Gregg Fisher had been at the company for more than ten years and was fully vested in the company's ESOP plan. Someone else said that once you become fully vested in the ESOP plan, you are untouchable. HR cannot get rid of those employees who are fully vested, because the company could be slapped with a lawsuit. Someone else said that the company would rather sacrifice its employees to the Black Death than risk a protracted lawsuit. Someone else said the company hated paying lawyers almost as much as it hated paying its employees. Everyone got a good chuckle out of that one.

Gregg Fisher works in software. Some people believe that the software department is actually a coven of witches posing as a software department, but this has not been verified.

Someone else said that it only looks like Gregg Fisher is typing at his computer, but upon closer inspection, he is not pressing down on the keyboard at all. His hands hover over the keys, and he makes typing gestures, but he isn't really typing—he is pretend typing. It freaked people out.

Someone said that they noticed a strange quiet down in software—an unnerving quiet. Someone else said they once went down to software and they swear there was an odd odor and a kind of fog emanating from somewhere, possibly the same smelly smoke that Gregg Fisher's old Chrysler K-Car or Plymouth Sundance used to emit. That made people nervous. They had hoped Gregg Fisher's old car was dead and gone. Someone suggested that maybe Gregg Fisher had zombified his old car and cut out the zombified tailpipe, burying it within the walls of the software department. That way, it would periodically emit thick, smelly smoke to keep people from coming down to complain about the screwed-up software.

Someone else said they wouldn't be surprised if one day, the software developers stormed the upper floors of the building and ripped out the beating hearts of some of the employees. Some people thought that marketing might get their hearts ripped out first, and then someone else said that it was impossible because no one in marketing had a pulse. Everyone got a good chuckle out of that one.

Someone wrote an anonymous note to HR about how no one in software ever seemed to be at his cubicle. They left out the part about Gregg Fisher and his pretend typing, because most people were resigned that HR couldn't do anything about Gregg Fisher. Soon afterward, HR sent out a company-wide e-mail saying that all anonymous notes sent to HR must be signed by the employee writing the note and co-signed by the employee's manager. The e-mail said the company mandate for the next fiscal year was transparency, and that this applied to all kinds of correspondence, even confidential correspondence. This incensed most of the employees, except, someone noted, Gregg Fisher, whom this person saw lean back in his Aeron chair after reading the e-mail, a smug satisfaction gleaming in his muddy brown eyes. Someone else said they didn't believe it was possible they could despise Gregg Fisher more than they already did, but because of his reaction, they put him in an entirely new category of people they hated—a category where you put people like Hitler and Osama bin Laden and Dick Cheney and, now, Gregg Fisher.

That person ultimately left the company under strange circumstances. After that, some people thought that Gregg Fisher and Dick Cheney might be cousins.

Someone offered to stay late one night until Gregg Fisher went home, and then burn sage over his desk, his Aeron chair, his keyboard, and maybe, if he forgot it, his commuter mug. This person hoped to clear out the demons that Gregg Fisher must have summoned from the depths of Hell. Someone else said that they didn't think that sage-ing Gregg Fisher's cubicle was going to help. Someone said they didn't think that Gregg Fisher ever left the building; that they were working late one night, and when they went down to the parking lot, they saw Gregg Fisher's Pontiac Vibe with its lights on. They didn't stop to see if Gregg Fisher was in the car or not, but either way, it was spooky.

It made people nervous to think about Gregg Fisher hiding in his Pontiac Vibe late at night in the parking lot. Someone else mentioned that they might want to consider driving a wooden stake through Gregg Fisher's heart, but someone else said they didn't think that Gregg Fisher had a heart. Everyone got a good chuckle out of that one.

One Halloween, someone put a cut-off chicken head on the hood of Gregg Fisher's Pontiac Vibe. This wasn't the first time someone had played a prank on Gregg Fisher. Someone once put fake plastic vomit on Gregg Fisher's Aeron chair. Someone else once wrote a love note to Gregg Fisher and signed it, "A Secret Admirer." Everyone got a good chuckle out of that one. But someone said that this time, it wasn't a joke, and that the powers that be had gotten serious about getting rid of Gregg Fisher. Someone said that certain executives were sufficiently freaked out by Gregg Fisher and decided to take matters into their own hands. Someone else said that a decapitated chicken head on the hood of Gregg Fisher's Pontiac Vibe was a bad omen, a harbinger of evil. Others thought that creating a hostile work environment for Gregg Fisher would only cause a lawsuit. Still others thought that Gregg Fisher himself put the chicken head on the hood of his own car to scare people.

Someone else said they were in the parking lot when Gregg Fisher noticed the chicken head on the hood of his Pontiac Vibe, and that he had pounded on the hood and howled like an animal. That same person said it looked like Gregg Fisher was crying his eyes out. Someone else said it could have been an act, and that Gregg Fisher must have known that someone was watching him. They had heard that Gregg Fisher was an Eagle Scout and had been taught to hear at a higher frequency than most humans. Most people agreed that Gregg Fisher would know on an unconscious level whether he was alone in the parking lot and whether to feign crying.

There was a lot of discussion about whether Gregg Fisher could hear in his mind when other people were talking about him. That made the people who did a lot of talking about Gregg Fisher nervous.

One day, someone went down to software and didn't see Gregg Fisher at his desk. Some thought that Gregg Fisher might have gone out on stress leave. Someone said that if Gregg Fisher could provide a doctor's note with a valid reason as to why he couldn't be at work, he could be paid up to 75 percent of his salary for three months. Someone else said that even if Gregg Fisher did go out on stress leave, the company would have to keep his job available to him for six months. After that time, Gregg Fisher would have to be offered a job within the company, even if it was a job in a different department and for lower pay. Someone said there was no way that Gregg Fisher would accept a job in a different department, because then he would have to learn how to actually type, not just pretend type. Everyone got a good chuckle out of that one.

Someone else thought maybe Gregg Fisher was sick with the flu that was going around the software department. Still others thought that Gregg Fisher caused the flu going around the software department, and that he was told to stay home until he stopped being a carrier for diseases. People breathed easier that night when they went down to the parking lot after working late and did not see Gregg Fisher's Pontiac Vibe. Everyone felt a lot safer.

After a week, someone saw a new person sitting in Gregg Fisher's cubicle. Shortly after, HR sent out an e-mail to all employees stating that Gregg Fisher had to leave the company for an indefinite period of time due to a personal matter. Everyone wondered what that meant. Someone said that Gregg Fisher caused personal matters for others, and that was his personal matter.

Someone else said maybe he had to take a leave of absence to take care of his aging parents. Someone else said they didn't believe that Gregg Fisher had parents in the traditional sense; that they wouldn't be surprised to learn that Gregg Fisher had sprung from the head of his father, like Athena from Zeus. That person had paid attention to the mythology unit in freshman English.

Some people asked around the software department, but no one seemed to know anything or would divulge anything if they did know. Someone else heard Gregg Fisher had left the building one Friday evening and never came back, not even to clean up his cubicle or retrieve his commuter mug. Some people wondered what happened to the commuter mug. They thought that it had probably been incinerated. Others believed that management confiscated the mug to have the contents tested, because management was building a criminal case against Gregg Fisher and that the mug was considered evidence. It made some people nervous to think about what was inside Gregg Fisher's commuter mug.

Someone thought Gregg Fisher, as unlikely as it may sound, was having an affair with someone in upper management and that when the relationship went south, Gregg Fisher was paid off to leave the company quietly and without his ESOP shares. This scenario was quickly shot down. No one could picture anyone human touching Gregg Fisher, let alone anyone having a torrid affair with him. Someone else said, "Who said anything about upper management being human?" Everyone got a good chuckle out of that one.

Someone stayed late one night and saged Gregg Fisher's old desk. As that person went down to their car, they noticed Gregg Fisher's Pontiac Vibe in the parking lot with the headlights off. Even though it was against this person's better judgment, they looked at the Pontiac Vibe and noticed an item on the hood. Upon closer inspection, they realized that it was Gregg Fisher's ponytail, cut off above the scrunchie, lying in a wet, straggling heap. The person was so freaked out that they couldn't remember driving home. Everyone who heard the story the next day was scared. Someone thought that Gregg Fisher had most likely cut off his own ponytail in a self-destructive rage and then put it on the hood of his own car to scare the people who were working late. Most people walked around the hallways of the office somewhat tentatively that day, looking out of the corners of their eyes for the ponytail to show up again, perhaps in an unlikely place like the women's restroom on the third floor or in the cleaners' storage closet.

Someone else who stayed late the next night thought that they saw Gregg Fisher's Pontiac Vibe parked in the circular entranceway of the building. They thought they saw Gregg Fisher himself in the driver's seat, his muddy brown eyes staring, unblinking, as though he were dead. For a long time, no one stayed too late at work, for fear that Gregg Fisher's undead body and filthy Pontiac Vibe were stalking the parking lot. Then HR sent out an e-mail saying they were installing new lights in the parking lot. Someone said that it was due completely to Gregg Fisher's undead body, while others disagreed.

Several people said that Gregg Fisher had started to infiltrate their dreams, that he would show up in the strangest places—like in a meadow or a cityscape or a park bench—and that he would sit and stare at the person in an accusatory way. In some dreams, Gregg Fisher still had a ponytail. In others, he was bald. It made people uncomfortable to see Gregg Fisher in their dreams.

Some of those people who dreamed about Gregg Fisher had to go out on stress leave. HR sent out a company-wide e-mail stating that if someone was out on stress leave, they were not allowed to attend the monthly departmental parties. Those parties were reserved for those employees still working. Many people thought that Gregg Fisher had tried to attend the monthly software barbecue and was turned away. It made people nervous to think about Gregg Fisher trying to attend the software barbecue, although most people believed that if Gregg Fisher wanted to rip out and eat the beating hearts of most of the employees in broad daylight, he would do it and no one would be able to stop him.

Someone else said it still smelled funky in software, despite Gregg Fisher's absence. But that person was not vested in the company's ESOP plan and was ultimately forced to leave under strange circumstances. Most people know better than to discuss Gregg Fisher openly anymore. Most people recognize that Gregg Fisher's powers were even greater than they could have imagined, and that they could risk certain death by talking about Gregg Fisher or even by thinking about him. Most people ignore the smell in software, or they have stopped going there altogether. Most people, when leaving the building after working late, band together in small groups by the elevators for safety. When they get to the parking lot, they walk quickly and with purpose to their cars. They do their best not to notice Gregg

Fisher's Pontiac Vibe, even dirtier than usual, parked in the employee lot, headlights off.

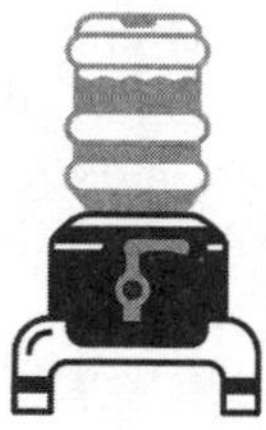

Northanger Abbey

HERE'S THE FIRST LINE OF MY NEW NOVEL:

"Once upon a time, there was a boy who was born into a wealthy family."

But it is all a big ruse that the family was wealthy, a ruse that, if you continue reading, will evaporate right in front of your eyes. But for now, suffice it to say that the family was wealthy. At least, that's what you, the reader, are led to believe thus far, as you've only read the first sentence. Do not worry: this is not to mislead you; it's a source of dramatic tension later on in the story for the reader to think that the family was wealthy, when in fact they were just pretending to be wealthy for appearance's sake.

Appearances vs. reality is going to be a major theme in this novel, so major that it is going to be one of the book club discussion questions in the back of the book.

So the family, let's call them the Snooty-Richersons, pretended to be rich for a variety of reasons that will be discussed in detail later on in the novel, which is my latest, which is to say my most current novel or, more specifically, my first novel.

I am writing my first novel!

One reason the family pretended to have money was so that when they sent their son to the fancy private school, Northanger Abbey, the rich kids at the school wouldn't make fun of him, calling him names like "scoundrel" or "fat ass."

It's been duly noted by me, the author, that Northanger Abbey is the name of a novel by Jane Austen, but rest assured, the use of the name "Northanger Abbey" in my novel has nothing to do with Jane Austen. In fact, who's even read *Northanger Abbey* in the last twenty-five years? Look at me—I'm writing a novel, and I've never read *Northanger Abbey,* even though I was supposed to in high school, or maybe that was *To Kill a Mockingbird*. Believe me, it hasn't kept me from writing. One should always follow his dreams, or in lieu of dreams, take the free "Writing the First Novel" webinar offered by the Learning Annex. Don't ever let naysayers keep you down, even if your family practically throws you out of the house for refusing to attend anger management classes.

To clarify, this novel takes place in the 1980s because everyone loves the 1980s—that decade is simultaneously cool and retro for the millennials and yet nostalgic for Gen Xers like me. I was in the bank the other day when they started playing the song that was my high school graduation theme, "Dancing on the Ceiling." I guess they figure that most people cashing checks will have fond memories of high school, but that song plunges me into despair.

Upon looking over my work, I think that it may sound inauthentic for boys to call other boys "scoundrels." Calling someone a "scoundrel" seems kind of hokey, even for the 1980s. Nowadays, you can get in trouble for using the word "scoundrel," even in casual conversation. One example would be when you call your local bank teller Robert "a scoundrel" because he questions why you are trying to cash a check with your mother's name on it.

Here's a book club question:

"Is it fair to be banned from a bank just for taking action because one's mother seems to no longer understand the concept of a weekly allowance?"

So the kid's parents, Fred and Delores, are pretending to be rich so that they can send the kid—his name is Franklyn, or no, better yet, Ralphie—to Northanger Abbey. They mortgage their middle-class home in suburban Chicago so that they can come up with the money for Ralphie to attend Northanger Abbey, which is located in Lake Geneva, Wisconsin. Fred works as an actuary for State Farm Insurance, which isn't a bad job, mind you, but it's a boring job, a job Fred got roped into years earlier when he knocked up Delores while they were both freshmen at the University of Illinois at Urbana-Champaign and had to get married. Fred is one of those guys who is genuinely smart, and if he had had better luck and was generally savvier about birth control, he might have invented the Internet or cell phones. But alas, no, he and Delores had to get married, courtesy of Delores getting pregnant and her churchy parents. This will all come out in the middle of the novel, which will be devoted to Fred and Delores's relationship. There will be some killer sex scenes, so you might want to warn some of your churchier book club members before you all dive in.

You might also want to warn some of the more softhearted book club members that Delores's story is a very sad one. If you've ever cried watching a commercial for Cymbalta, then you will probably bawl your eyes out reading my novel. I don't want to give too much away, but let's just say Delores meets a very unhappy end due to an extreme case of psychosomatic Alzheimer's disease. If that doesn't make you want to turn to page one right now, I'm not sure what would.

There are going to be sections of the book written from Fred's point of view and sections written from Delores's point of view and sections written from Ralphie's point of view. The Delores sections are going to be very florid, because Delores is a very florid personality. She is pretending to be a rich housewife, but in reality she is an abstract painter consumed with the idea of painting the outside of the family house so that it blends in with its surroundings, like camouflage. If Delores had her way, you would drive down the street and not even notice the house because it would blend into the neighboring forest preserve. If you didn't know better, you might think that

Delores was a little bit nutty, but you'd be hard-pressed to say that she suffered from a degenerative brain disease, even though that's what she wants you to think so she can get attention. Anyway, you'll learn more about Delores's secret past and tragic present later on because they are integral to the plot. You'll also learn that Delores used to make a killer vegetarian lasagna back in the day before she conveniently "forgot" how to make dinner.

Another note about Northanger Abbey, the fictional school: it's not an abbey at all, but when the school was being built, the rich jerks who commissioned it decided to call it Northanger Abbey, because one of them was supposed to read *Northanger Abbey* in his high school English class and never did, but he liked the name because it sounded all fancified and snobby. Not to give too much away, but it's going to turn out that Fred's great-uncle Jason was that rich jerk. It may not seem like a big deal right now, but it's all going to fit together like pieces in a puzzle.

Here's a possible book club question:

"If you were one of the three people on record who read *Northanger Abbey,* what did you like about it? Or are you just a poseur and a snob like Fred's great-uncle Jason?"

Metaphors are going to be very important in this novel. Keep your eyes open for a plethora of metaphors to hit you smack on the ass!

Anyway, back to the action: Delores, Fred, and Ralphie drive up to Lake Geneva in their Chevy Caprice Classic station wagon. Ralphie is stuck sitting in the wayback because all of his stuff—including the tennis racket, golf clubs, and ascot collection that Delores bought because she thought Ralphie would need them to impress the cultivated kids at Northanger Abbey—is taking up most of the backseat. Cars are passing the family on the highway and kids keep flipping Ralphie the bird because he is a gawky teenager sitting in the wayback, which looks, if I might say, incongruous.

There are going to be many incongruous parts of this novel. You are also going to find lots and lots of dichotomies: there will be a dichotomy between rich and poor, between majorly drugged out and sober, between defenseless sons and withholding parents, between the idyllic appearance of upper-middle-class success and the chaotic reality of a dysfunctional family with loads of debt and lots of shameful secrets. If dichotomies are your bag, then you are going to love this novel.

In the middle of the drive, Fred pulls off the interstate at a rest stop. He tells Delores and Ralphie that he needs to use the men's room, but he really doesn't need to use the men's room. Fred needs to think, alone, away from his family. Dads tend to spend a lot of time in the bathroom when they should be out taking responsibility for their sons' stunted emotional growth. Instead, he's in the stall, contemplating how his life got so messed up. See, Fred didn't tell Delores this because she would kill him, but he just got laid off from his job at State Farm. It's the 1980s, and everyone is into conspicuous consumption and shoulder pads, including Delores, who, because she had a kid so early on in life, feels like she deserves all kinds of payback from Fred, even though getting pregnant was both of their faults. Delores usually told Fred when to pull out during intercourse, but that one time she got carried away and forgot to give him the signal.

Delores has expensive tastes, which is incongruous because an abstract painter would seem to be an earthy type of person and someone who wouldn't be interested in material things, but you haven't met Delores! She's an enigma. Delores likes fur coats—big, expensive furs from Saks Fifth Avenue. It's the 1980s, and fur coats are all the rage. PETA hasn't made many inroads into the celebrity culture yet, so fur is still fine by most people's standards. Fred bought Delores a beaver coat one year, which cost him a bundle, but Delores said that she preferred mink and expects one this Christmas, which is only a few short months away.

Fred wipes away the sweat from his brow in the men's room. He's sweating because it's the end of August in northern Illinois and humid as hell, but also because he's nervous about coming clean about his financial situation. The other big thing we learn in this scene is that Fred lied to the Northanger Abbey bursar in a telephone conversation just that morning, saying that he is bringing the check for Ralphie's first semester. In reality, Fred doesn't have the money, even with the Snooty-Richerson suburban home in hock.

Here's another question for the book clubs:

"What is the etymology of the word 'bursar'?"

We learn in a later chapter that it was Fred's fault that he got laid off because he was having an affair with his secretary, Ms. Donna Fulsome, who wasn't disgusted by giving blow jobs the way Delores was. Apparently someone in the typing pool overheard Ms. Donna Fulsome talking dirty to Fred and blew the whistle on their affair. State Farm didn't need a sexual harassment lawsuit, so it let Fred go, even though he was great at his job and super smart to boot.

This is compelling! What is Fred going to do?

My next novel is going to be about what could have happened to Fred if he hadn't screwed up and gotten Delores preggers. I think it might be about Fred creating a superweapon and battling aliens who threaten to dominate Earth. Or it could be a novel about Ralphie accidentally discovering Fred's secret second family (the Fulsome-Snooty-Richersons) and the recurrent Cymbalta abuse that discovery engenders.

Just as we are wondering what will happen to Fred in the men's room, the novel jumps ahead and follows Ralphie, now a junior at Northanger Abbey. It's clear that Ralphie is attending Northanger Abbey, but it's unclear how that was possible, given that Fred didn't have the money to pay for it. But that's not our focus here, because Ralphie is in the midst of an existential crisis. This will be made obvious to the reader by a hundred-pound weight gain since we last saw him at the rest stop on the way to start his freshman year and also his more-than-recreational drug use. He's getting Ds in his gen ed classes and is considering transferring to Carl Sandburg High School in his hometown of Orland Park, Illinois.

Here's another question for the book clubs:

"How might Ralphie's life have been different (weight-wise, drug-use-wise, emotional-health-wise) if his parents weren't shallow yuppies with addictive personalities?"

At this point, there will be a lengthy digression discussing the pros and cons of transferring to Carl Sandburg High School. Here are a few examples:

> PRO: Carl Sandburg High School has tons of extracurricular activities, such as sports and student-run organizations like the Key Club. Key Club members raise money for the school through fund-raisers, like car washes and candy-bar sales. Being involved in the Key Club prepares one to be a good citizen and even has the potential to help a person get into the college of his choice.
>
> CON: Carl Sandburg High School is full of douches.

In the rest of the chapter, through Ralphie's rambling first-person narrative stream of consciousness, the reader will deduce that Fred and Delores may have both been killed in a car crash. It's hard to pinpoint because Ralphie is all jacked up on quaaludes. We can also infer that Ralphie is the resident adviser of the Quiet Residential Plaza, also known as the "nerd dorm," because in the middle of his delusional rant—which, by the way, is occurring at three o'clock in the morning—one of the nerd freshmen on his floor, Janet Goodwin, comes running into his room. Janet says there's an emergency and that Ralphie better get to her room, stat! Running on pure adrenaline, Ralphie picks his fat ass up off the floor, toppling the three-foot bong he bought while on spring break at South Padre Island earlier that year, and leaps into action.

Janet Goodwin will later figure in a romantic subplot with Fred and Ms. Donna Fulsome, but I don't want to give away too much just yet.

This is exciting! How about the complication of Ralphie being whacked out on drugs and forced to act in an emergency? Here there will be a long description of how the Count Chocula T-shirt Ralphie is wearing stretches tightly over his large gut, and we can practically hear the *swish swish* his dung-colored corduroys are making as his thighs rub together as he races down the dark but tastefully appointed hallway.

Delores should have known that corduroy is one of the least forgiving materials you can find on planet Earth. If Delores hadn't been such a self-involved narcissist, then she would have been invited to play bridge with the other mothers in the neighborhood and thus would have known that bullies like Matt Kelly, who lived next door, specifically targeted boys dressed in Wrangler cords.

Ralphie gets to Janet's room all out of breath and finds Fred sitting on her bed, crying. Whoa! No one expected Fred to show up at this point! We thought Fred might be dead, but given that he is sitting on Janet's bed, we can see for ourselves that he is alive, and apparently Ralphie's earlier rant was just a hallucination or a delusion. Or was it?

It turns out Fred is having an existential crisis of his own back home in Orland Park and thought he would drive up to Northanger Abbey to visit Ralphie on a whim.

"It's the middle of the night, Dad," Ralphie says.

"Is it?" Fred says.

"Yes. The middle of the night," Ralphie says.

"Night. Ah, night," says Fred, "the darkest part of the day."

The best dialogue is always pulled from real life, right? You can't make this shit up.

As you might notice, this is a very obscure conversation in which Fred and Ralphie talk about nothing, but there is a ton of subtext regarding Fred and Delores's crumbling marriage and Ralphie's self-destructive tendencies learned at the knee of his father. How else do you think boys learn about quaaludes? From their cheating, quaalude-popping dads of course!

Here's another book club question:

"Ever heard of the 'iceberg'? You're in a book club—you must have read Hemingway. If not, why not?"

Here's another one:

"Does hearing the song 'Dancing on the Ceiling' make you wish that Lionel Richie was your father instead of your real father?"

This inscrutable dialogue will be very important because Fred will tell Ralphie, in a not-very-easy-to-comprehend manner, that he is leaving Orland Park because Delores divorced him in a fit of pique. This too will all be explained in the series of florid chapters written from Delores's florid point of view. The reader will find out that Delores took the bus to New York City to try her luck in the New York art scene, Andy Warhol and that shit, and over the course of the novel, she becomes a huge success in the folk art community. Too bad she now claims that she can no longer remember her fame and fortune, or, for that matter, her son's name.

This novel has something for everyone. It's got black humor, dichotomies, metaphors, drug usage, suburban angst, semiautomatic weapons, corduroys, an iceberg, and lots, lots more.

At this point, there is going to be a "meta" chapter about how the novel *Northanger Abbey* is a satire of gothic novels from the eighteenth century, like *The Mysteries of Udolpho*. This part of the book is going to pander to literary types who join book clubs to show off how smart they are because they were comp lit majors at Brown like forty years ago.

In an ironic twist, instead of reading and discussing the book during the book club get-togethers, one of these literary types, let's call her Mrs. Schnell, spends that time in the kitchen, attempting to seduce her best friend Delores's son, Ralphie. Mrs. Schnell, while old as dirt, wears an intoxicating perfume that makes saying no to her sexual advances extremely difficult.

This chapter will have surprising plot machinations, like when a confused Delores breezes into the kitchen and, thinking she's in the bathroom, pulls down her pants and starts peeing on the linoleum, all while Ralphie is being fellated in front of the fridge. Again, churchy book club types beware!

According to Mrs. Schnell, "meta" novels are hot right now and one has to try to stay current on literary trends, even if one has never heard of *The Mysteries of Udolpho,* let alone knows what a gothic novel is. Unless you're a sixty-something retired high school English teacher who still gives a great blow job, you would probably have no idea. I sure didn't! And I still don't.

Don't let *The Mysteries of Udolpho* keep you from reading my book!

Here's another book club question:

"If Delores claims that she pissed on the kitchen floor because she thought she was on the toilet, does she suffer from early onset Alzheimer's or is she just a crazy bitch?"

Another chapter is going to address how there is medical evidence that eating certain types of foods can help people with "brain diseases" remember important facts about their lives that they claim to have forgotten. I find that eating sardines makes my brain work better. Sure, the checkout people think I'm a little bit nutty for buying sardines ten tins at a time, but I have found that sardines, more than any type of food, give me the kind of creative energy I need to keep writing. I personally love sardines in tomato sauce, but I have been known, in a pinch, to eat the kind in olive oil. My favorite way to eat sardines is with saltines. I keep sardines and saltines in my cupboards at all times. But that's my creative process—an interesting fact for the book clubs. You heard it here first, because once I become a famous novelist, sardines are going to be the new food favorite that everyone is going to want to eat. A sardine company might even pay me to become its celebrity sponsor.

Another possible book club question:

"Which do you like better: sardines in tomato sauce or sardines in olive oil?"

Here's another one:

"Are you plagued by dreams where your mother serves you what is supposed to be her delicious vegetarian lasagna but it ends up morphing into a pile of sardines? What do you think that means?"

It's going to come out in a later chapter that Ralphie is going to end up fighting a lifelong addiction to Hershey's Bars. Mrs. Schnell, the English teacher who oversaw the Key Club, never checked Ralphie's candy-bar inventory. Ralphie began to hear strange, urgent voices in his head, telling him to eat all his Key Club bars, and after a while, people started calling him "fatty fat-fat" and "pig face" and "buffalo ass."

As an adult, it is going to be impossible for Ralphie not to pig out on Hershey's Bars whenever he encounters them at the grocery store when he is picking up sardines.

I hope that buffalo ass Matt Kelly is homeless somewhere, sleeping under the el tracks.

I've just figured out how Fred could afford to send Ralphie to Northanger Abbey! Major plot twist: Fred will find out from an episode of *Antiques Roadshow* that a grandfather clock he inherited from his great-uncle Jason is worth a million dollars, and that's how he and Delores will have the money to send Ralphie to Northanger Abbey. Done and done. Fuck Carl Sandburg High School.

CON: Carl Sandburg High School throws totally lame twenty-year reunions that are not worth the fifty bucks borrowed from Delores's Social Security check. No one even remembered me. Not even Matt Kelly.

Here's something I just wrote:

"'Hey, pig face! You have a fat ass!' said Matt Kelly.

[I just decided that Matt Kelly is going to be the name of a fictional student at Northanger Abbey.]

"'Is that the best you can do, scoundrel?' Ralphie said, hoisting his three-foot bong over his head and smashing it on top of Matt Kelly's dung-colored hair. Matt Kelly fell over, a large red gash apparent in his big, putrid head.

"'I guess it's all over,' said Ralphie, watching as Matt Kelly's brains ran out over the plush white Stainmaster carpet that came standard in every dorm room at Northanger Abbey."

There's been a murder at Northanger Abbey! I did not see that one coming. As a writer, you never feel good about killing off a character, but if it's in service to the story, then so be it.

I'm going to change Ralphie's name back to Franklyn. It's been rough going through life being named Ralphie. I don't know what my parents were thinking. It's extremely selfish to saddle a child with that kind of baggage.

Here's another question for the book clubs:

"Why is Delores still in a book club when she claims she can't even read anymore? Is she faking dementia to avoid making amends for all the messed-up shit she and Fred dumped on Ralphie growing up? Did she ever love him? Discuss."

If Mrs. Schnell comes to the book club meeting tonight, I may invite her back to my bedroom to show her the first and only page of the novel and then I'm hoping to bang the hell out of her. I think she'll be impressed that despite all that has happened to me, I've turned out pretty good. I'm writing a novel, aren't I?

This is going to be the last line of my novel:

"Franklyn's ghost dusted off his own grave. He sighed and disappeared into the darkness."

My novel will have something in it for everyone. Believe me.

New Directions

EMPLOYEES:

There is a matter of some importance that the executives would like to share with you. As leaders of a company that was voted one of the five hundred most transparent companies in the San Fernando Valley (*Westways Magazine*, September 2009), we pride ourselves on addressing any type of situation.

As most of you know, the software department has been busy prepping for the first-quarter release of MPM 3.0, the newest iteration of Production Solutions' continuing quest for better payroll-processing software. MPM 3.0 will be a game changer, providing our clients with sleeker and hipper ways to process payroll than ever before. But when Managing Director Deirdre Dempsey went down to the second floor last Friday for her regular meeting with our programmers, she found the department empty. She checked the kitchen and the patio, then asked Martin from facilities to check the restrooms on each floor. No software personnel were on the premises. Managing Director Dempsey says that she didn't find this altogether strange, given that the developers sometimes keep odd hours. She was, however, "weirded out" by the silence, so she sent what she describes as a "forceful" e-mail to Product Manager Jim Smalley.

That e-mail went unanswered, and at three o'clock she went back down to software with a "full head of steam" and again found no one. This time the lights, which are on a motion detector, were out, indicating that no one had been there in six hours.

Since that time, HR has made contact with the families of all software-department members. It seems they all left for work on Friday, but have not been heard from since.

We are investigating this phenomenon to the very best of our abilities. The sheriff's department has been alerted, as has the FBI. This is not, we stress, an emergency. According to law enforcement, mass disappearances are not uncommon. Often one person will decide to take the day off and others will follow suit, in "senior ditch day" fashion. We trust in our officials and believe they are doing all they can to locate the missing software department. We will continue to give you updates as they become available.

EMPLOYEES:

Some of you may have heard that the clothes the software-department members were wearing at the time of their mass disappearance were found in the dumpster near the facilities shed across the street. This is unsubstantiated. No clothes were found in or around the dumpster. In fact, Bob Ferrara's nebulizer was still running when the department was discovered to be missing, so we can only assume the team left in a great hurry, with no time to strip. As soon as we have any new information regarding the software department, we will alert you.

EMPLOYEES:

Some of you have expressed concern about the absence of several members of the accounting staff. Do not worry. They have all been located at their homes, where they are suffering from pinkeye, courtesy of Doris McClellan's daughter, Amy. In response, the executive team is considering canceling Bring Your Daughter to Work Day.

If your coworkers are out of the office, do not immediately assume the worst. Unless you are told otherwise, coworker absences are due to illness, paid time off, stress leave, or some other nonthreatening reason.

Please note that the search continues for the software department, and that the executive team realizes that, since we are primarily a software company, we cannot function without a software department. We are meeting about this every day.

EMPLOYEES:

A new e-mail address has been created for questions regarding the software-department situation. Please e-mail softwarequestions@prodsol.biz. Do not ask HR or the executives for updates, as we are extremely busy. Thank you for your cooperation.

EMPLOYEES:

Production Solutions is going through a challenging time, and we appreciate your efforts to remain calm. Some of you have managed to complete your work in a timely and error-free manner. A shout-out to Rachel Kaiser, in particular, who answered more calls this month than anyone else in tech support—more than three hundred calls! Congratulations, Rachel! A gift will be on its way, pending management approval.

Others, however, have not been as successful at regulating their anxiety. Please note that e-mailing the software-questions address several times a day with speculative "leads" will not rectify the situation any faster. Nor, for that matter, will hounding your managers about when MPM 3.0 is going to be released. It is also unhelpful to hit the Ignore button on your phone, leaving your fellow tech-support representatives to answer your calls. (Congratulations again, Rachel.)

And let it be said too that neither kicking over the soda machine in the break room nor spray-painting a pentagram on the wall is the optimal way to handle stress. Instead, consider these options: talk to your coworkers about the latest sport scores during your state-mandated fifteen-minute break; take a yoga class before or after work; remove your headset and take deep breaths at your desk.

We must continue to act in the best interests of our clients and the company. Thank you for your attention.

EMPLOYEES:

In answer to a frequently asked question, our HMO does not currently cover yoga classes. It also does not cover chiropractic or acupuncture. We will bring these items up with our insurance provider during negotiations next year.

EMPLOYEES:

It is imperative that we not let our competitors or news outlets learn about our current challenges. To that end, an electronic legal agreement is up on the intranet, which you must sign electronically as of five P.M. today. It is vital that all employees sign the waiver. It is a simple one-click signature. Once you have done so, a Starbucks gift card will be distributed to you by your manager. The only way to obtain the card is to sign the waiver. If you have any questions about the waiver, the software department, or anything else related to this current obstacle to our company's success, please direct them to softwarequestions@prodsol.biz.

EMPLOYEES:

It has been brought to our attention that Starbucks is not accepting some of your gift cards. This was an oversight. New gift cards will be distributed to those who have complained and whose electronic-waiver signatures have been verified. Please do not e-mail the software-questions queue with theories about the lack of funds on the Starbucks cards, and do not listen to anyone who tries to convince you that Starbucks has something to do with the disappearance of the software department.

It has further been brought to our attention that some employees do not drink coffee. Per their requests, we are looking into using Costco gift cards in the future. Please note: Starbucks gift cards cannot be redeemed at Costco.

EMPLOYEES:

Many of you have inquired as to why new software developers have not been hired during such a crucial time. Please know that the HR department has been working tirelessly to hire temporary workers. Although we reside in the software-development capital of the nation, finding new staff has proved trickier than you might expect. Despite our best efforts to keep the software department's disappearance out of the public eye, news has trickled out to our competitors and to news outlets, making it challenging to attract top talent. We are investigating this security breach to the best of our abilities.

EMPLOYEES:

We are pleased to announce a partnership with a Vientiane-based firm that will send over temporary programmers from Laos. The firm promises that its workers will "power up" quickly, get the work done, and then "power down" and leave the country immediately. These temporary employees will not drain our 401(k) plan, nor will they be given spot raises, bonuses, or Starbucks gift cards. They will also not be allowed to park their rental cars in the parking lot until we can have the missing software department's vehicles towed.

The Laotians will arrive next week, and we're thrilled to have them continue the software department's work creating user-friendly software that offers real-world solutions. We'd appreciate it if you would make the effort to introduce yourselves. As managers of one of the fifty most engaged companies in California (*Westways Magazine*, June 2011), we trust that our employees will welcome the outsourced workers with open arms. Instead of using your break to go across the street for a Big Gulp, why not take a quick field trip to the second floor and extend a friendly greeting? Incidentally, *"Sa bai di, mu pheuon"* means "Hello, friend" in Lao.

EMPLOYEES:

Due to employee demand, we have created a list of FAQs regarding the team arriving from Laos:

1. What is Laos?
Laos is a country in Southeast Asia. For more information, please consult: https://en.wikipedia.org/wiki/Laos.

2. When you say that the Laotian team will "power up," does this mean that they are robots?
No.

3. Is Production Solutions paying for the team's meals and housing?
Production Solutions will pay them a housing stipend. The team has also been issued Costco gift cards.

4. Will the Laotian team receive health benefits?
Health insurance for the new team is being covered by the outsourcing firm. We believe their co-pay for the urgent-care clinic on Hollywood Way is ten dollars.

5. Will any current employees be terminated?
All Production Solutions employees are classified as "at will," meaning they can be terminated at any time. Please refer to page IV 3.2–3.6 in your employee handbook for more information about what it means to be an "at will" employee.

6. How long will the Laotian team stay?
In the event that the software department resurfaces, the Laotian team will remain until the FBI closes its investigation, then will "power down" and leave. If the software department fails to resurface, the team will stay on until the new release date for MPM 3.0, which is the last day of the third quarter. The executives have been in meetings about the missed first deadline for the release of MPM 3.0 with our clients, who have been extremely understanding about the circumstances.

EMPLOYEES:

It has been brought to our attention that a sign reading FOR AMERICANS ONLY has been hung next to the urinals in the first-floor men's room. It was neither placed there by facilities nor authorized by management, and has been taken down. Please note: Posting unauthorized placards in a public building is a misdemeanor in the state of California. Anyone found doing so will be prosecuted.

EMPLOYEES:

Although the temporary software developers were expected to begin work this morning, they have not yet arrived. We do not know the reason for this delay. But do not worry: the welcome potluck is still on. Please enjoy Luz Endoso's famous pansit noodles and the many other goodies in the second-floor conference room.

EMPLOYEES:

The Laotian team's absence is still under investigation. In answer to a frequently asked question, the Laotian overseas firm is not, we repeat *not*, a front for terrorist activities. We have consulted with the U.S. Department of Homeland Security, and in no way do they believe that our building has been targeted for a terrorist attack. Production Solutions has asked Robert, Doc, and the other security guards to be extra vigilant, just in case.

We ask also that you stop e-mailing the software-questions queue, as it is full.

EMPLOYEES:

We have been informed by the firm in Vientiane that the Laotian software team decided to reject our offer. Please do not blame them for their choice. In business, it's never personal. Many factors went into their decision. We will continue our search for new software developers to help us grow our business and build our dreams.

EMPLOYEES:

Please do not speculate as to why the team from Laos rejected our offer. It is not our concern if they decided to "power up" with Entertainment Options instead of us, and anyway, this rumor is unconfirmed. Please do not spend time worrying about things that are out of your control. Concentrate instead on doing the best job you can. Help a client by answering your phone instead of letting it go to voice mail. Brush up on knowledge-base articles about previous versions of our software. If you need to, stretch quietly at your desk. Thank you in advance.

EMPLOYEES:

In answer to a frequently asked question, yes, Mike Heno took executives from the Laotian firm to a Los Angeles Kings game. It is part of Mike's job as an HR manager to entertain people who can help us solve our staffing issues. Mike was as surprised as anyone that the firm rejected our offer at the last minute. The Laotians reportedly enjoyed the game, and one of them even purchased a foam finger. The executive team has every confidence in Mike and the rest of the HR group. Please do not e-mail Mike directly, as he has gone on leave.

EMPLOYEES:

Please do not e-mail the executive team with questions about the deposit paid to the Laotian company. We are working hard to secure the return of those monies, as well as the Costco gift cards that were sent in advance.

EMPLOYEES:

We understand that you are feeling stressed, and we appreciate that you are weathering the storm as well as can be expected. But we must request that you please, per the confidentiality agreement that 58 percent of you have signed thus far, refrain from discussing the missing software department with outside parties, whether they are family, friends, or news outlets. Having crews from local stations, CNN, and Fox News perpetually parked outside the main entrance is not good for business. Already, many of our clients are refusing to send their staff to our building to pick up their payroll checks for fear they may disappear.

As Franklin D. Roosevelt said so famously, "There is nothing to fear but fear itself." It turns out that he was right. Try to not be afraid; it rubs off on others. Now is the time for all of us to pull together and continue to wow our clients in the face of adversity. The best thing you can do is to excel at your job.

We are still planning to hold midyear reviews.

EMPLOYEES:

We would like to take a minute to acknowledge the suggestions we've received from you all over a frankly difficult past few months. Here are a few of your many "out of the box" ideas for new directions in which to take the company:

1. Turn the building into a day-care center. Use employees (nicer employees) as caregivers.

2. Repurpose the building as a Banana Republic outlet. Offer employees 40 percent discounts.

3. Transition the business into a soy-candle boutique called Sea Whispers. Offer employees 40 percent discounts.

4. Convert the building into a jai alai fronton. Use employees to run concession stands and larger employees (Doc, Robert, and Cookie) as security.

While the executive team appreciates your suggestions, we remain committed to our current business model. Thank you for understanding.

EMPLOYEES:

Because we value your creative spirit, the executive team is excited to announce a new slogan contest! While we're very fond of our current slogan—"Production Solutions: WOW!"—we believe our valued employees can do even better. E-mail your ideas to slogan@prodsol.biz. Participants will receive tickets for a raffle to win a 7-Eleven gift card and some lottery scratchers.

EMPLOYEES:

We have to discuss a sensitive situation with you. As some of you know, Deirdre Dempsey, whom we have long esteemed for her perfect attendance record, has been out of the office since Monday. Rest assured, Deirdre is not missing. When you see her next, you will notice that she is wearing a wig.

This is because she has been diagnosed with stress-related alopecia. She is under the care of our HMO's doctors and will hopefully regrow her hair in time. Please try not to ask her too many questions, as this will worsen her alopecia. Please note also that this occurrence, while unfortunate, is completely unrelated to the disappearance of the software department. The FBI is diligently following every lead.

EMPLOYEES:

Due to this year's challenges, it is unlikely that anyone will receive a merit raise following the next performance-review period.

EMPLOYEES:

For those of you who have inquired, the executive team has not had time to judge the slogan contest. We have been extremely busy dealing with various local, state, and federal investigations, not to mention the loss of most of our business. For those who sent nasty e-mails regarding our unresponsiveness, shame on you. We have hardly slept the last several months. We would ask that you show a bit more courtesy. Or perhaps you were born in a barn? You know who you are.

EMPLOYEES:

Some of you have heard that Project Manager Jim Smalley appeared to his wife in a dream. He was dressed like a Boy Scout and was selling boxes of Trail's End Popcorn door-to-door. When his wife asked him where he was and what had happened to him, he smiled and said, "Support our troops." Then she woke up.

To this end, please support our troops for all their efforts by purchasing Trail's End caramel corn from Doris McClellan's son, Travis, who will be in the office on Thursday. Do it for the software department, wherever they may be. Please note that Travis will be carrying only twenty dollars in change.

EMPLOYEES:

Due to managerial leaves of absence, e-mails to software-questions@prodsol.biz will no longer be read. For answers to your questions, please refer to the new FAQ list below:

1. Is the disappearance of the software department still a mystery?
Yes.

2. Why have new software developers not been hired?
This is proprietary information.

3. What will happen to the company's long-term profitability in the wake of the software disappearance?
This is also proprietary information.

4. Third quarter has come and gone. What happened to the hard release date for MPM 3.0?
Again, proprietary.

5. Was the software-questions e-mail queue shut down because it was a portal to another dimension?
Improbable. Also, proprietary.

6. Where is my manager?
Many managers have taken paid stress leave. Others are not

returning e-mails or phone calls. Try to exercise patience with the managers who remain.

7. Will Production Solutions be in existence for the long haul? Who of us is in existence for the long haul?

8. Why did facilities remove all the ficus trees from the lobby? The ficus trees were not performing to the best of their abilities. If you have additional questions, please write them down for next year's town hall meeting, which has yet to be scheduled.

softwarequestions@prodsol.biz—Out-of-office auto-reply:

Please join us in the second-floor conference room at three o'clock. Neither cake nor coffee will be served, but we wanted to gather all remaining Production Solutions employees and commend you for your loyalty nevertheless.

If you are reading this e-mail, congratulations. You have braved much insecurity. Since most of the facilities department has defected to Entertainment Options, even getting into the elevators these days entails great bravery. While we no longer have the funds to pay for gift cards, bonuses, or salaries, there is something to be said for togetherness. If any of you would like to say a few words, tell a joke, or sing a song, even a sad one such as "Danny Boy," you will be welcome to do so. We no longer care if you can carry a tune. It was wrong of us to snicker at James Lalange's karaoke version of "Purple Rain" at last year's holiday party. It's the small cruelties that add up, in the end.

If you want, we can reminisce about the old days. Remember Luz Endoso's world-famous pansit noodles? The semiannual bingo tournaments? The comforting, low-level hum of Bob Ferrara's nebulizer?

On second thought, let's not talk about those things anymore. Let's talk about something else.

Winners and Losers

THERE ARE TWO KINDS OF PEOPLE IN THIS WORLD: winners and losers. Winners know on a primal level that they are heads and shoulders above losers. This winner was drinking a beer, watching the game at Bumpers, when he noticed an average loser crying like a ten-year-old girl while mangling the lyrics to "Faithfully." The winner asked the loser, whose name turned out to be Joe Grant (typical loser name), what the problem was. Joe replied that his girlfriend had dumped him. The winner thought he would cheer Joe up by buying him a beer, which turned into Joe and the winner getting shitfaced on shots of Wild Turkey. Winners are generous with their time and money.

When the winner tried to pay the tab at the end of the night (typical winner move), the bartender informed him his debit card was declined. The winner told her that made no sense. He'd asked his parents the day before to please deposit forty dollars into his account, and he was pretty sure they had come through. The bartender ran the card again without success. The winner tried to explain how bank deposits can take extra long to clear when they are made from a different time zone. Winners are very tenacious.

Winners attract losers at bars because winners give off an air of self-confidence. Sometimes they go a step further and allow losers to believe they are winners. That's why the winner let Joe Grant pay the $72.50 bar tab. He even let Joe Grant buy him a Munchie Meal at the Jack in the Box across the street. Winners are gracious that way.

When Joe says his call center job at the cable company is going to lead to a manager position one day, the winner nods in agreement even though he knows Joe will be wearing a headset for the rest of his life. As Joe drones on about how he's taking management courses through the University of Phoenix, the winner sips his Coors Light and changes the subject to football. The winner knows it is inconsiderate to take the wind out of a loser's sails. Losers need to hold on tightly to their dreams, no matter how ill conceived they might be. Winners recognize that losers are losers for life.

The winner spends a lot of nights at Bumpers listening to Joe's grandiose plans. Sometimes the winner has to tune Joe out. The winner has found that doing whip-its in the parking lot beforehand really helps with this. It also loosens the winner up. One night, a couple of hot girls came in, and the winner definitely had his flirt on. Winners are courageous. The winner was a little loopy from all the whip-its, but he was game when the girls started doing shots of Jägermeister and even later when they switched to tequila. Winners roll with the punches.

The winner vaguely remembers one of the girls saying something about teaching kickboxing at the Y. The winner remembers telling her that even though he had never tried kickboxing before, there was no way a girl would be able to take him down. Winners know that girls lack the kill factor, and they aren't shy about saying it.

The winner can't exactly remember what happened next, but somehow he ended up splayed out on the Trivia Whiz machine, looking down at his bloody tooth. Even winners occasionally forget that doing shots after eating nothing but a bean and cheese burrito all day is not the formula for success. Winners try to learn from the few mistakes they make.

Loser Joe Grant left the winner moaning on the floor while he sucked face with the hot kickboxer, and then had the temerity to drive off without the winner. Joe had driven the winner to Bumpers, because the air-conditioning in the winner's Toyota Tercel was making that funny noise again. Losers have no idea how hard it is to find a cab at two o'clock in the morning on a Tuesday night. But winners are resourceful. A winner will limp after an off-duty bus for two blocks before giving up the fight. A winner is willing to sleep on a bus bench, only to be woken up by a man in a tinfoil hat claiming dibs.

Winners don't judge others. It's against their nature. Winners believe that with a tremendous amount of work and intestinal fortitude, anyone can become a winner, even though for most losers, it's impossible. Once at a barbecue, this winner met a loser from Denmark who wanted to become president of the United States. Winners know full well that a Denmarkian, or whatever a loser from Denmark is called, cannot become president. Why? Because it's the law. And who creates laws? Winners.

This winner was not about to call the Denmarkian loser a fucking idiot. That would be mean, and winners reserve meanness for extreme situations, like being stuck behind someone driving a Prius. The winner instead flashed the loser from Denmark a friendly smile. Winners know that a smile is an effective way to disguise feelings of rage.

Winners don't set out to make big impressions, but they often do. The loser will no doubt e-mail his friends back home in Denmark about the charming winner he met. He will write about how terrific a listener the winner was. He will write that the Euro-socialist claptrap he was spewing did not seem to disgust the winner. In fact, the winner was disgusted, but winners have learned how to transform disgust into enthusiasm.

The winner munched on his hot dog and suggested that one day the loser from Denmark could become a loser governor of California, like Arnold Schwarzenegger. The winner chose not to mention that he'd personally move to Nevada if a commie Scandinavian was ever elected and allowed to legislate his pinko ideas. To paraphrase the winner Aaron Sorkin, losers cannot handle the truth.

If the asshole from Denmark had half a brain, he would have recognized that the discussion was getting out of control. He should have guessed that something was brewing when the winner's cheeks turned bright red and the vein on his forehead began to bulge. Instead, the loser kept talking about how wonderful the health coverage is in Denmark and about how unfunny Will Ferrell is. Paying special attention to social cues is the trait of a winner, not a loser.

Winners are often the greatest guys at barbecues because they know when it's time to leave, even though their exit may seem kind of abrupt. Winners know to disregard comments they hear from others, like "Dude, why are you being such a douche?" and "Hey, bro, can't Jürgen have an opinion?"

Winners understand it is better to storm out of Joe Grant's backyard, tossing a Coors Light into the pool on the way, rather than come to blows with a Denmarkian loser. Brawling with a man in clogs is behavior unbecoming of a winner.

Winners do not attend many loser barbecues, because for some reason they do not get invited more than once. You might think being a winner would be lonely, but it's not. Winners would rather chat with other winners about *Match Game* on the Game Show Network message boards than attend a loser barbecue anyway.

Winners realize that losers need to talk incessantly about their own neuroses, like how they are convinced that they are their own worst enemies. When a loser says that the universe has big plans for her if she could just get out of her own way, the winner only pretends to listen. In reality, the winner suspects there is no way in hell this loser is ever going to get out of her own way, or, for that matter, anyone else's, since her ass has gotten so huge.

The winner has laser-focused insight into this loser's pathetic brand of self-delusion, because this loser is the winner's older sister, Pam.

Growing up in New Jersey in the 1980s, the winner struggled with cystic acne throughout his adolescence and endured years of cruelty from many losers. You would not expect though that the worst insults came from his very own sister. Using hurtful nicknames like "Captain Crusty" is behavior typical of a loser. So is ruining the winner's high school graduation by telling him his purple tassel "matched his zits." Some losers are bigger bitches than others.

When Pam showed up at Thanksgiving last year wearing plus-sized jeans, the winner didn't make a crack about her weight gain. When Pam's thirteen-year-old daughter, Gabriella, texted all the way through dinner and didn't look up once, the winner didn't comment on how rotten a parent Pam turned out to be. The winner instead was quietly satisfied that Pam would always be relegated to the universe of losers. This loser universe includes Pam; Pam's ex-husband; and her current boyfriend, Ira, whom she met at an Overeaters Anonymous meeting. Ira seems like an okay guy, but a winner has too much self control to ever need a twelve-step program.

That night, Pam cornered the winner in his old bedroom in their parents' house. She said that her OA sponsor (loser) told her that she needed to make amends for making fun of him. The winner said he forgave her. He even allowed Pam to give him a hug. Even though the winner would have rather vomited up his own intestinal tract than to have to physically touch Pam, he hugged her anyway. That's what winners do: they feign love when what they clearly feel is blistering hatred.

When the winner hugged Pam, he noticed that her hair smelled like flowers. Her arms, although pale and doughy, gripped him with a kind of fierce tenderness. It reminded the winner of when he was little, how Pam would sometimes give him a horsey ride on her back. He would bury his head in her long, dark hair and beg her to go faster, and she would, bucking up and down until the room began to spin. As the walls whipped around him, it would seem as though the world was made up of only the winner and Pam. As Pam hugged him, tears sprang to the winner's eyes.

Crying feels unnatural to a winner. The winner hadn't cried since the day in fourth grade when he discovered his guinea pig, Pee Wee, under the radiator. That's another mark of a winner—a high pain threshold.

Just as the winner feared he might break down and weep in front of Pam, he got a hold of himself. He forced himself to stop thinking about Pam's horsey rides and instead thought about the NFL Draft. Sure enough, he started feeling like his winning self again. Winners have trained themselves not to feel their feelings for too long, as it has caused them problems in the past, occasionally with law enforcement.

When Pam finally let go of the winner, she said that she wished he could meet a nice girl. She said that if he started attending AA meetings and got himself into therapy, maybe someone would want to date him. She said that he needed to expand his hobbies beyond drinking Coors Light to excess and binging on porn and Doritos.

There are certain things that both winners and losers enjoy. Those things include, but are not limited to: baseball, Coors Light, Doritos, and porn. It's how winners experience these things that make the difference. Winners watch porn for hours because it's fun, not out of desperation. They drink Coors Light and eat Doritos because it is an enjoyable way to spend a Saturday night, not because they are lonely.

Trying to make losers understand this can sometimes get a winner into trouble. Pam refused to see any difference and started in on one of her trademark bitching sessions. The urge to knock out Pam's permanently whitened teeth did not register the way it had in the past. No, the winner took Pam's bitching as sisterly advice, even though the winner would never take advice from Pam, no matter how many amends she tried to make. The winner knew that taking a loser's advice was like accepting an invitation to stay free at a Hawaiian resort, courtesy of a time-share company. You'd have to be an idiot to do it.

A winner never lets anyone pull the wool over his eyes, particularly a loser sister who still owes him a birthday present from when he was eight. But winners don't dwell on the past.

Winners welcome change. They can pick up at a moment's notice and jet off to their next adventure. Two years ago, this winner decided that he would move out to California to try to make it as a screenwriter in Hollywood. The winner was extremely excited about this idea, even though Pam pronounced it "really, really stupid" at the time. The winner argued that he was highly prepared for this career. He had recently obtained his BA in comparative literature after twenty-two nonconsecutive quarters at Rutgers. He had taught English at a middle school in Livingston for four months. Naysayers like Pam might ask. Had the winner ever written a screenplay before? No. Did he know anyone on the West Coast? He had one friend, Joel Raschow, whom he saw on LinkedIn was a nutritionist/life coach in Burbank, but he hadn't spoken to him since Hebrew school, so no. Did all this stop the winner from embarking upon what promised to be an experience of a lifetime? No. Did the winner want to be stuck teaching *Dandelion Wine* to a bunch of sarcastic eighth grade fucks for the rest of his life? No thanks, Pam.

The winner packed all his belongings into his Toyota Tercel and set a course for Hollywood. Winners do not let little setbacks get them down, like when the Tercel blew a tire before he even got on the turnpike. Or when the winner was arrested at a Steak 'n Shake off I-55 for public drunkenness. Or when the winner had to ask his parents to wire him gas money just outside of Reno. These minor problems paled in comparison to the future, where anything could happen.

The winner finally made it to Hollywood, and only had to sleep in his car for two nights before finding an apartment on Craigslist. Once settled in, the winner checked out some screenplay books from the library and started reading. Winners will stop at nothing when pursuing their dreams. Losers might find it concerning to blow their entire savings on Robert McKee's Story Seminar at the LAX Embassy Suites, but winners keep their eyes directly on the prize.

While the winner's loser roommate, Chad, worked outside the Grauman's Chinese Theatre in Hollywood as an Elvis impersonator, the winner spent every waking moment on his screenplay. Winners can be extremely focused.

The winner would wake up, brew a pot of coffee, read and reread several chapters of the Robert McKee book he'd bought at the seminar, take a short break to update his status on Facebook, read more, eat a 7-Eleven bean and cheese burrito, make more coffee, and then hang out at Bumpers' happy hour with Joe Grant. He also spent time outlining the characters for his screenplay. It's what those in the business call a four-quadrant picture—that means there's something in it for everyone, for winners and losers everywhere. There's a handsome hero who makes hilarious fart jokes, and a hot bisexual chick with an enormous rack, and a cute animated talking car named Sparky that turns out to be a serial killer. It's a film that will be full of raunchy humor, hot sex, terrifying violence, and major superhero action.

The winner would have liked to work full-time on his screenplay, but his dwindling funds and lack of parental support forced him to seek some type of employment. He started working outside the Grauman's Chinese Theatre, dressing up as Chewbacca. Did the winner enjoy his work? No. Did the winner want to put on a polyester Wookiee costume and then stand in the stifling heat for five hours on Tuesdays, Thursdays, and Saturdays? No. Did it scare the winner to be chased around by the clinically insane losers who hung around the courtyard? Yes, often. Did the winner enjoy being told by loser *Star Wars* fans that they found his performance inauthentic? No. Did the winner feel good about having to perform sexual acts on random losers while dressed as Chewbacca just to pay his share of the cable bill? Does the winner really have to answer that?

Did the winner ever have moments when he wished he were someone else, someone whose life was not completely fucked up? Did the winner ever want to throw his hands up in despair? Did the winner, in his darkest hour, worry that perhaps he was not a winner at all, but in fact a loser?

No, he did not.

Was the winner surprised when the lit agent from WME, whom Joe Grant introduced him to, actually read his screenplay? Was he surprised that the agent loved it and wanted to sign him as a client? Was the winner surprised when the agent sent the screenplay out to Will Smith's people, and Matthew McConaughey's people, and Channing Tatum's people, and that the response was phenomenal? The winner can't say he was surprised.

Winners realize that life is a marathon. They understand that hard work pays off. After the winner sold his screenplay, he moved out of his crap apartment in Van Nuys and now rents a bungalow in Hermosa Beach. The winner no longer has to drink at Bumpers' shitfest happy hour, although he shows up there once in a while to buy Joe Grant a beer. A winner's ship may come in, but the content of his character remains the same. Some winner said that.

The winner's life has of course changed. Nowadays, the winner works out with a personal trainer four days a week. The winner has lunch meetings with other winners.

Winners like John Stamos and Michael Bay. Winners like the guy who produced that Disney Channel show with Miley Cyrus.

Winners don't have to drink Folgers coffee anymore. They can go to the hippest coffee bars in Silver Lake and drink coffee that has been filtered through a Japanese coffee sieve. Winners can make their dream of a full head of hair a reality. In some other ways, though, the winner's life remains the same. As it turns out, winners in L.A. also consume a ton of porn and a lot of beer, although Doritos, not so much.

A winner can have his personal assistant, Geoff, get him reservations at Cut on any given Saturday night. He can force Geoff to work late researching eco-friendly dry cleaners and vegan Tahitian resorts so that the winner can take his hot new vegan model girlfriend on vacation. Winners might appear to be hard-asses, but that's only because most losers cannot tell the difference between hard-ass-ness and someone who has paid his dues and deserves all the successes coming to him. Pam still won't acknowledge that the winner makes more money in a week than she makes in a year. But winners do not gloat.

Pam had told the winner he would never make it in Hollywood and would come crawling back to New Jersey "like a little bitch" in two months. But the winner pursued his dreams anyway. So we come to perhaps the most important difference between winners and losers. Winners have perfected the art of waiting. They don't panic when the hard times come and they have to dress like Chewbacca. They do not suffer in vain. They have a higher purpose. They know what awaits them, on earth as it is in Heaven. Winners have the patience of saints.

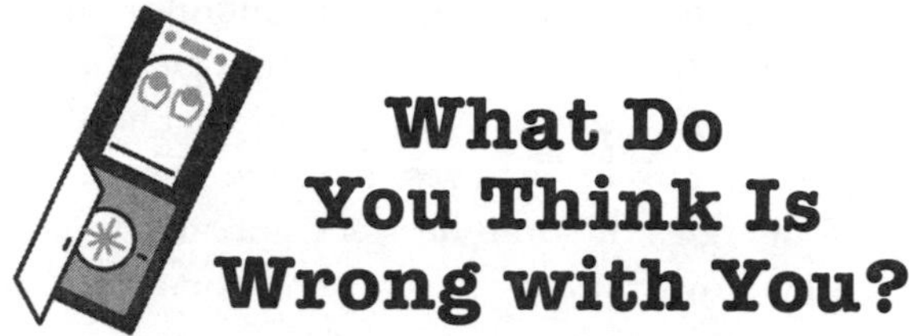

What Do You Think Is Wrong with You?

YOU CHECK YOUR INBOX AFTER YOUR SMOKE break. You have been sent an Outlook invitation from Amber for a meeting this afternoon at five P.M. Five P.M. is a late hour for a sit-down. A concerning hour. You hope this sit-down doesn't have anything to do with the incident from this morning. You cannot afford to be shit-canned. That would be extremely bad.

Maybe you are just going to get written up. That wouldn't be great, but it wouldn't be the worst thing. You haven't gotten that many write-ups. You try to remember: Did you get written up when you forgot to log a week's worth of phone calls? Did you get written up when Amber caught you watching *Weird Science* on your phone instead of logging in to the queue? How many write-ups did William get before they shit-canned him? You can still see William crying while packing his *Stars Wars* Lego collectibles into a box. Then Doc, the security guard, ejected him from the building. You take a deep breath. Don't get spooked just yet.

You decide to do some proactive research about the company's shit-canning policy. You dig around your desk drawers for the employee manual they must have given out at new-hire orientation. You don't find the manual, but you do find a Chewbacca Lego figurine that William must have left behind. You decide to make finding the manual your top priority after answering the phone. Stick a Post-it note on your monitor so you remember to look for it. Wait, put the Post-it somewhere else. You don't want Amber to see the Post-it on your monitor and think you are looking for the manual. She might get suspicious. On second thought, don't worry about it. She's always got that glazed look in her eyes, and she hacks so much because of allergies, it's like her face is ready to cave in. She could keel over at any second, and then who would care about your Post-it?

You try to recall if Savannah from HR said anything about the shit-canning policy at new-hire orientation. Okay, the orientation was six months ago, but you must be able to remember that far back. Think hard. You were hungover from the buy-one-get-one pitcher promotion at Bumpers, but you can sort of see the orientation happening in your mind's eye. You have a vague memory of Mandy announcing to everyone in the support center, "Bruce and I are going to new-hire orientation." You definitely remember that Mandy was wearing a red dress with black tights that day. But after that, you confess, things get a little fuzzy. Did you attend the new-hire orientation or did you blow it off and go to Jack in the Box? Were you at the orientation but asleep with your eyes open?

You used that excuse once back in Boy Scout camp. You had received a care package from your mom that included a *Dynamite* magazine with Kristy McNichol on the cover. You were supposed to be playing capture the flag with Cabin Jayhawk, but instead, the camp nurse found you and the magazine in the bathroom. When she found you, you played dumb and said you didn't know how you got there. You must have fallen asleep with your eyes open. You'd read in *Ripley's Believe It or Not* that it's a real thing.

The magazine was confiscated, and Mom and Dad had to drive up early to take you and R.J. home. They told R.J. that you were being sent home for poor knot tying.

"Why should I have to leave camp early just because Bruce couldn't tie a sheepshank? It isn't fair!" R.J. whined the entire car ride home.

If you can remember that conversation from thirty years ago, then you should be able to remember new-hire orientation, BOGO pitchers or not.

You decide to ask Mandy if she remembers your being at the orientation. Then you immediately reconsider. Amber doesn't like it when the reps talk to each other when they're on phone coverage. It could be cause for a write-up. You think about IM'ing Mandy instead. You also want to see if she has the manual handy.

Are you concerned that you can't remember your new-hire orientation? Or going through the drive-thru at Jack in the Box? Of course. Of course it is concerning to have large gaps in your memory. Of course it is concerning to find a bag of curly fries in the front seat of your car and zero recollection of how it got there. But you do not have the time to worry about it just now. You need to be concerned about keeping your job. That is your top priority. But don't forget to answer the phones, because that is also your job.

There's got to be a way to spin the incident to Amber in the sit-down. You could always blame the client. Everyone knows how grouchy the clients are. Even the managers make fun of them. Every time you walk by Amber's half-office, she's in there with Deirdre and Gary, chuckling about a complaint a client wrote on a survey. Clients are the reason everyone in the support center, managers included, drinks too much. You've seen the managers chug down BOGO pitchers at Bumpers. You've also witnessed Amber do shots, which gets a person way drunker than just beer by itself. Amber isn't stupid. She has to understand that the client, Sharon someone, caused the incident by being super mean to you. The clients pressure us to solve problems quickly and efficiently, but that's not the way things work around here. Like Amber says every morning in our scrum, "Efficiency is subjective."

Amber needs to know that you take your job seriously. Before the sit-down, you should take a moment to review the Levels of Service we are supposed to provide. Make this your top priority.

> Service Level 1: The responder team answers the phone. We are the first line of defense with client issues. We answer calls courteously. We do not use slang or unprofessional language. Example: "Hello, client, how can I help you?" is appropriate. "Damn, girl! What's up?" is not. We ascertain the issue by asking, "Client, what are you trying to accomplish?" Numbers are usually involved, but don't let that intimidate you. Never tell the client that you have no idea what they are talking about. Never suggest that the client get a less boring job. Most important, do not tell the client that you are only allowed to stay on the phone with them for a maximum of 5:30 minutes.

Service Level 1 requires critical thinking skills. Daydreaming about Mandy can make critical thinking difficult. Don't think about Mandy and her black tights. Mandy's black tights have nothing to do with Level 1 Service.

> Service Level 2: If after 5:30 minutes, you can't figure out the issue, then you need to escalate the no doubt very complicated case to the escalation team. The escalation team is made up of two people, LaGreta and Rose. Do not tell that to the client, though. The clients are supposed to think there are legions of people available at their disposal. Don't ever say, "Either Rose or LaGreta will get back to you." Say, "Someone from the escalation team will contact you." Don't worry if the clients put two and two together eventually when only Rose or LaGreta ever contact them. This is a Service Level 2 challenge. Stay out of it.

Amber keeps track of responder team members' performance. If they escalate issues that should have been resolved in Service Level 1, Amber calls them into her half-office for a sit-down. The first thing Amber does in those sit-downs is ask, "I'm just curious—why do you think you're here?" She gets pretty mad if you don't have a good answer. When Amber gets mad, her face looks like it is falling in on itself, and then you know you are in trouble.

Example: Amber called you out when you escalated a case that was ultimately fixed by the client restarting his computer. Amber said, "The escalation team has a lot to do. We need you to be able to convey an easy fix like restarting a computer without passing it on to the next service level." You replied, "I'm as shocked as you are. The client just wasn't making himself clear." You did not tell Amber that you couldn't pay attention to the client because of the conversation going on around you. Mandy was talking about signing up on Match.com and you wanted to hear what she was saying.

Amber then retold the story for like the fiftieth time of how she started out on the responder team, just like you. She too had to answer phones, and sometimes she didn't know the answers or could even understand the questions the clients were asking. But she persevered. Using Wikipedia, she researched how to effectively listen to clients. "If you are ever unclear on what the client is asking for, Bruce, one trick you could try is repeating his question back until you fully understand."

Amber's skill set is being able to make the clients feel satisfied, even if their issues aren't ever fixed. She was the finest critical listener the team had ever had. That's why she was promoted to manager.

Amber said, "Bruce, I understand that critically listening to a client can be a real challenge, but you need to improve your skills. Otherwise, we may need to have an sit-down with Gary." Gary is the senior manager, but he's mostly in charge of taking clients to baseball games.

He's rarely in the office, so you weren't too worried, but then Amber pulled out a piece of paper and pushed it across her desk. It read "Verbal Disciplinary Action." She gave you her pen and watched while you signed it. Then Amber smiled.

"I know you have it in you to be a fantastic member of the team. We just need you to be proactive—to care a little bit more. Can you do that?" You didn't tell Amber that you didn't think you could possibly care more. Instead, you gave her a little salute, like you did at camp when the nurse caught you with Kristy McNichol.

> Service Level 3: Software development: No one in the support center knows much about this service level. It's very mysterious. If the escalation team can't solve the client's problem, then software needs to get involved. No one has ever personally spoken to anyone in software. They usually roam around in packs, clogging up the tables in the courtyard. Some of them have been imported from a place called Bangalore. Others are just regular white guys who play Hacky Sack out in the parking lot.
>
> Occasionally, you will answer a call and the client will say, "My issue was escalated to software." In that instance, it is policy that you transfer that call directly to Amber's voice mail. Responder team members are never to speak directly to clients who have had their issues escalated to Service Level 3. Once software gets involved, it is out of our hands.

Amber will be impressed that you have such a strong handle on the service levels. It may soften her up a bit.

You could also tell Amber that the client, Sharon somebody, was rude to you, not the other way around. You could say that Sharon whoever had a complex issue with her software that required additional research. Tell Amber that per Service Level 1 policy, you informed Sharon that you were going to escalate her problem to the escalation team. When she asked when they were going to call her, you said that you had no idea because that team is always super busy.

You could say that Sharon flew into a rage and called you a not-so-nice name. That is a lie, but in an alternate universe, it might have happened that way. Wait, don't pass the buck on to the escalation team. Amber created the escalation team and she might get defensive. Just say that Sharon called you a not-so-nice name and hung up on you. That works better. Write this all down on a Post-it note. Remember to grab the Post-it when you go into Amber's office for the sit-down so you can read off it. That way, you can tell Amber you've fully documented the incident. But don't mention that you documented the incident on a Post-it note. She won't like that.

You could always decline the Outlook invitation and tell Amber you are sick. You could say you caught the respiratory infection that everyone has been passing around. Say you have to leave early so that you don't infect your teammates. That might give you some extra time—a day, maybe—to avoid the inevitable. You could at least kick back and have a few frosty pitchers at Bumpers. You try to log in to the accruals portal to see how much paid time off you have. You can't take any more time off if you don't have the days. You can't afford them docking your pay. You don't want to piss off Neil by not being able to pay your share of the gas bill like last month. Even though Neil says he's not sure how it happens, you'd better believe that when he gets pissed at you, he encourages his incontinent cat, Millie, to wander into your bedroom.

You realize you've forgotten your accruals portal password. You need to go in person to HR to get them to reset it. No, don't do that. Don't let anyone in HR see you. If you're getting shit-canned, you'll know it the second you walk over there. If Savannah won't make eye contact with you when you walk in, you'll know something bad is going down.

Example: Jeannie, a longtime member of the responder team, twisted her ankle in the stairwell and went out on a workers' comp claim. Now, if anyone ever mentions Jeannie's name near an HR person, they give you the stink-eye. Workers who go out on workers' comp claims are not welcome, in the stairwells or anyplace else. You made the mistake of asking in the last department meeting, "Hey, when is Jeannie coming back?" and the managers looked like that guy in accounting who had had a heart attack at his desk last year. Amber sucked in her cheeks even harder than usual, giving her face a weird concaveness.

IM Savannah about getting your accruals portal password reset. Try to get her to do it fast. This is delicate territory. If Savannah gets suspicious, then HR may get Amber to do the sit-down with you immediately. Avoid all this bullshit—just remember what the portal password is. Maybe it's the same as your Match.com password, Brucealmighty68. Try that one.

You forget about answering the phones. You need to figure out what to say to Amber about the incident. Ask yourself Amber's question, "What do you think you did wrong?" Or is it, "What do you think is wrong with you?"

During the sit-down you should act very nervous and upset. This will make it hard for Amber to discipline you. You remember this from the camp incident. Your parents didn't punish you, but your mother did immediately cancel the *Dynamite* magazine subscription and, to this day, has never sent you another care package.

You could tell Amber that you are not sure why, but you may have called the client a not-so-nice name. Tell her you got that respiratory infection everyone else has been passing around. Tell her that you were feeling simultaneously hyped up from too much DayQuil and free Tuesday bear claws and yet woozy at the same time, and you thought you should splash some cold water on your face. Just as you were about to get up, your phone rang. You have to answer the phone; that's your job. So you answered it even though you didn't feel well. But you are a team player. Everyone says that about you—remind Amber that she herself mentioned it as one of your strengths in your midyear review.

You could tell Amber that the client, Sharon whoever, was mean as a snake from the start. She cut you off while you were greeting her, and she refused to give out her last name. When you asked what the issue was, she replied, "Per usual, your dumb-ass software isn't working." Tell Amber that the client's attitude threw you off even more than the respiratory infection, but that you remained professional. It is one of your goals this quarter to work on being more professional. If you remind Amber that she set that quarterly goal for you, she'll pretend to remember.

Tell Amber that you tried to follow what the client was saying, but that you were too light-headed to be an effective listener. Being a more effective listener is another goal Amber set for you—throw in that reference so she'll know you have been trying to listen more effectively.

Do not tell Amber that when that bitch Sharon said, "Bruce, you are obviously a moron. Is it too much to ask that you know how to do your job?" that you responded, "Is it too much to ask you to shut up, you chicken fuckface?" and hung up on her. Amber would not like that. Calling someone "chicken fuckface" is not exemplary Level 1 Service.

Another idea: What about if right before the sit-down, you create a diversion? Pull the fire alarm. Or better yet, ask to borrow Mandy's cell phone and, under your breath, call in a bomb threat to the building. Once the cops trace the call, all the attention will be fixated on Mandy for at least twenty-four hours. If the police ask you what you know about Mandy, say that the two of you were hired at the same time, but other than that, you don't know much about her. Do not say that, oddly enough, her thick ankles make you horny. Do not tell them that you signed up on Match.com to set up a date with her secretly. Say that she is a loner and keeps to herself. That will keep them interested for a while. No, don't do that, she'll remember lending you her phone. She might be mad that you incriminated her to the police and then she won't go out with you. Be vague if the cops ask you what she's like. Tell them you have memory lapses, sometimes involving Jack in the Box.

Maybe you should proactively call your parents to inform them about this possible impact to your finances. Tell them you realize it's been a while since you called, but that you've been very busy being a productive citizen. Say that you wouldn't ordinarily do this, but that you are in a dire situation and require additional funds. Tell them that you need a new set of sheets because Neil's cat peed on your bed. When your mother scoffs, resist the urge to call her a not-so-nice name. That will not help your cause. Plead your case more passionately than usual. Listen effectively to Mom and Dad's misgivings about lending you more money. Don't roll your eyes when Mom says, "R.J. never needed any help from us—he got that great job at Motorola right after graduation, and he's been working there ever since." Say that R.J. probably still wets the bed like he did at Boy Scout camp. No, don't say that. That will not help your cause. Fess up that Neil's cat isn't the real problem. Say that you may have violated an antiquated customer service rule at your company, and it's possible you might lose your job. If they ask, "So, what did you do wrong?" change the conversation. Say that the company is laying off everyone. Say that they will read about it in Monday's *Wall Street Journal*. No, don't say that. They might buy Monday's *Wall Street Journal* to see if you are lying. Say that the layoffs are being done in secret. Then cut to the chase! Say that $5,000 would be plenty to get you over the hump if you need to find a new job. No, make it $3,500. If they seem to be on the fence about lending you cash, think about those beer commercials with the Clydesdales that always get to you. You'll be bawling in no time.

When they agree to deposit $500 into your checking account, breathe a huge sigh of relief. Thank them and try to sound genuine. Say "I promise to make you proud." Pretend you don't notice that your mother hung up without saying good-bye. Don't think too hard about your father saying, "I love you, Bruce. Try to be good. Can you do that?"

This also might work: you could tell Amber that you are having personal problems. Tell her that you're in the middle of a painful breakup with your secret girlfriend, Mandy. That will shock her into submission. She may even have to leave the sit-down to tell the other managers the gossip right away. Tell Amber that you and Mandy chose to keep your relationship discreet. Tell her that the relationship began at new-hire orientation. Mandy looked at you from across the conference room table and something inside you surged: a thick, lugubrious swell of energy. Use a big word even if you don't know what it means—big words impress Amber. Say that after you and Mandy had that moment at the new-hire orientation, you joined Match.com. You did it because Mandy told everyone in the support center she was on Match.com. You joined so you could flirt with her without her knowing that it was you. Tell Amber that you made up a name and used a photo of your roommate, Neil, for your profile pic, but that the rest of the information you provided was more or less true. Although, you aren't from Dubuque, as "Bennett Sherman" says he is, but nobody checks on stuff like that. Mandy didn't.

It's almost five o'clock and Amber will be waiting for you in her half-office. Maybe you should take a more Zen approach to this sit-down. Try instead to focus on the beauty in the universe. Watch the hummingbirds that occasionally buzz around the patio when you are out there on your e-cigarette break. Take the suggestion to care more to heart. Consider what your life might look like if you were to become an effective listener. Picture yourself as a manager. Visualize yourself in your own half-office. Picture yourself laughing it up at Bumpers while sharing BOGO pitchers with the other managers. See yourself helping a misguided responder team member by offering him valuable feedback. See yourself making the decision not to shit-can him even though he probably deserved it. It's all about helping others reach their potentialities. Life doesn't have to be so desolate. Stop making excuses. Let the truth set you free. Dig out that *Power of Now* audiobook R.J. gave you for Christmas last year.

Tell Amber what really happened at camp. Tell her about how you snuck into the boys' bathroom in the main building while the counselors were busy shooing everyone out of their cabins to play capture the flag. Tell her that you hid the *Dynamite* magazine under your shirt. Tell her that it electrified you, feeling it folded against your skin. Tell her how you closed the stall door and sat down on the toilet. Tell her how beautiful Kristy McNichol was, how even now you sometimes fantasize about her tomboy jean jacket and feathered hair. But then tell Amber that you started to feel suffocated by the white walls surrounding you. How it dawned on you that you were merely ogling a photo while the real Kristy McNichol was out there somewhere in the world, probably playing tennis or drinking a glass of grape Kool-Aid. Maybe she wasn't even wearing her jean jacket. Tell Amber that you imagined what Kristy herself would say if she knew what you were up to. "You're disgusting!" she might say. "Your mother sent you this magazine because she thought you would get a kick out of the article about me. You were supposed to share it with R.J. Now, it's ruined. Bruce, what is wrong with you?"

Tell Amber that despite this distraction, you quickly exploded all over Kristy McNichol's feathered hair.

Afterward, you found that you were unexpectedly filled with an uncontainable rage. Tell Amber how, in a frenzy, you wadded the *Dynamite* magazine up into a ball and flushed it down the toilet. Tell Amber that the magazine got stuck and how the toilet began quickly filling up with water. And while all this was happening, you felt like you were the one being flushed down the toilet. As though you were the one being sucked through the camp's ancient pipes, attempting to gain traction to stop yourself, to keep yourself afloat. And as water from the overflowing toilet filled the stall, you began to cry, and the noise attracted the attention of the nurse whose office was down the hall. Tell Amber that the nurse knocked repeatedly on the stall door, asking, "Who is in there? What in heaven's name have you done?" Tell Amber that when you think about it now, you wish you had told the nurse how angry you were. Watch Amber's face fall in on itself as she grasps how angry you still are.

You run out of the building before Doc can catch you. Catch Mandy in the hallway on your way out and tell her that the Match.com date she is supposed to go on tonight is not with some guy named Bennett Sherman, but with you. No, don't do that. Just show up to the date and tell Mandy the truth: that Bennett Sherman is your roommate—no, that he's your brother. Tell Mandy that Bennett showed you her profile picture and that you recognized her. You told Bennett that you knew her from work, and that she was very good at customer service. Also that she is beautiful in a weird way. No, don't say that. It might freak her out.

Tell Mandy that Bennett Sherman got that respiratory infection that is going around and was too light-headed to go on the date. But you assured him that you would show up in his place, so that's why you're there instead of him. Mandy might cock her head the way she does when she listens to a client issue. She's definitely an effective listener. She may even let you buy her a beer. She may not buy that whole thing about Bennett Sherman, though. She might assume it was a big ruse to get her to go out with you. But maybe, before she makes up some story about having to leave to wash her tights, you can throw in about how you got shit-canned today because you called a client a "chicken fuckface." She'll probably laugh and say something like, "Oh my God, Bruce, that's ridiculous." And who knows, maybe you'll also find it ridiculous. Maybe you'll laugh too.

Back to Me

HERE'S THE GOOD NEWS, DR. SUSAN: I'VE MADE A real breakthrough since our last session. I was listening to a story on NPR yesterday about adults on the autism spectrum, and it made me realize I might be one of those adults. I'm not sure I recognize social cues. How else could I have not seen Bret was emotionally unavailable even after being so serious with him? Don't you think that explains a lot? Yes, I can see you're still with a patient. I just thought this was important. I'll come back...

...Can I start now? Okay. I also can't read facial expressions—it's a disease called prosopagnosia. It sounds made up, but it's real, I googled it. Turns out, I have four out of the five symptoms, including "perceiving inanimate objects as human beings." Remember how I told you about that one time when I kept staring at that hottie across the bar and licking my lips, only to find out later he was a Dance Dance Revolution machine? You chalked it up to my being high on whip-its, but now I think it's something more serious than that.

I can tell you're getting defensive, Dr. Susan. I'm the one who should be defensive! Who is the injured party here, you or me? After all the time we've spent together, I would think you would have noticed something screwy with my reasoning. I don't mean to be an asshole, but maybe you're not up on neuropsychology the way you should be. I can't be your only client suffering from a brain disorder. I mean, take that guy I walked in on—he was wearing a tie with shorts. What's up with that?

Okay, back to me. You should have said, "Stacy, you may need to see a specialist, because you're exhibiting signs that you're on the autism spectrum. Furthermore, Stacy, having a spectrum disorder may make it markedly difficult for you to properly assess a romantic partner, especially one who sounds to me like he is emotionally unavailable." Pretty good imitation of you, am I right? It's all my improv training. *SNL* tends to hire people who are good at imitations, so I've been working at it for years. It's only a matter of time until they call me in for an audition.

Let's be honest, I probably wouldn't have wanted to hear that I suck at picking boyfriends. I bet I would have scooped that ceramic unicorn off your desk and smashed it against the wall. But after I calmed down, I'm sure I would have seen the wisdom of your diagnosis and made an appointment at Cedars-Sinai to have them evaluate my brain. After all, Dr. Susan, this is my future we're talking about.

You don't remember who Bret is? I met Bret during my bartending shift one night at Duffy's. He kept looking at me and smiling. After a while, I went over because I thought he was cute and also to make sure he wasn't a Trivia Whiz machine. There was instant chemistry and we got friendly with each other, if you know what I mean. Just to be clear, I mean we ended up doing it. Oh, you got where I was going with that.

The next morning I woke up before Bret did and watched him sleeping. I couldn't help but picture the adorable faces of the children we might have together. If they were twins, I already had the names picked out: Morgan and Montserrat. Morgan I always thought sounded good for either a boy or a girl, and Montserrat is this girl in my beginner Groundlings class. She's not very talented and she wears those short shorts where half her butt is hanging out. All the guys in class seem to want her to play their hot girlfriend in improv scenes. But I like the name anyway.

At first, everything seemed fine with Bret and me. We hooked up like at least three more times. One morning, I asked Bret where he saw the relationship going. He looked a little uncomfortable, so I said, no pressure, he could think about it. I said I'd see him later, grabbed my shoes, and got out of his car.

That night, I baked my famous chocolate chip banana bread and left it at the front door of his condo. He never called to thank me. Later when I asked him about it, he said he got it, but that he wasn't eating real food because he was in the middle of a cleanse. Of course I believed him—why would my boyfriend lie to me? But clearly anyone who is not on the spectrum would have seen right through that excuse. Why didn't you alert me, Dr. Susan? You should have said, "Is it possible, Stacy, that Bret isn't looking for a relationship? And what kind of person refuses to eat homemade banana bread? Especially, Stacy, when it's baked with love?"

Now that I understand my prosopagnosia or whatever it's called, I've been dissecting the details of our relationship. It's becoming more and more obvious to me now that Bret was a jerk. For one, he never laughed at any of my hilarious stories. I know they're funny because famous comedians find them hysterical. I waited on Amy Sedaris once when she was hanging at the bar at Second City. When I told her about the time in high school when my choir director told me to go jump off a roof—so I did—Amy was apoplectic.

If Bret had ever come to my beginner Groundlings class to watch me perform, he would have seen for himself how funny I am. He was the reason I had all the VHS tapes of my improv shows in the 1990s converted to DVDs. If I don't say so myself, back in the day, I was a crack-up as the hot mom and the slutty girlfriend, and even when my teammates pimped me into playing the mute sister (which they did more than once).

Dr. Susan, you think I'm funny, right? Remember when you said, "Well, Stacy, you're definitely quirky, I'll give you that." I can play quirky just as well as I can play the hot mom. Quirkiness is definitely in my improv wheelhouse. I've been working on quirkiness for years for my *SNL* audition.

My last therapist, Dr. Rob, said that sometimes quirkiness could be a disguise for low self-esteem. How come we've never discussed my low self-esteem? Just so we're clear, Dr. Susan, I'm not paying you to placate me. I'm paying you to help me find a soul mate who will be a wonderful father to Morgan and Montserrat.

Bret never did watch my DVDs. He always had some excuse. Once when I called to see if he wanted to come over for a viewing party, his assistant told me that he had gone to the ER for a suspected case of meningitis. Of course, I ran right over to Cedars to make sure he was okay. The nurse said they didn't have a patient there by Bret's name. I asked if maybe he was admitted under a different name. I mean, I use aliases all the time. The nurse assured me that Bret wasn't a patient and told me to calm down. When I screamed that my boyfriend was in the middle of a meningitis attack and that the hospital had lost track of him, the doctor on call intervened and threatened me with a psych evaluation.

How come you've never suggested that, Dr. Susan? Is it because you can't tell the difference between someone who is quirky and someone who requires a psych evaluation?

When Bret showed up at Duffy's a few nights later, I was so happy to see him that I practically spit out my tequila shot. I said I hoped his meningitis had cleared up. He had an expression on his face that I couldn't place at the time, but knowing what I know now about facial cues, he was looking at me like I was crazy. Have you ever looked at me like that, Dr. Susan?

I didn't want to make waves with him, so I let the whole episode go, even though he didn't seem sick or weak or have any other symptoms of meningitis, which I googled.

By the way, I didn't know that a stiff neck was a symptom of meningitis—maybe I need to get checked out for that as well. I thought my stiff neck was due to all the time I spent giving Bret blow jobs in his car.

Dr. Susan, I've spent many years honing my craft—I know I'm talented. It's just a matter of time until my *SNL* audition comes through. Sometimes I get a little bit ahead of myself, though. Like the time I told Starleigh, my improv teacher, that I was ready to take the intermediate Groundlings classes. She told me, "Stacy, nobody is disputing the fact that you think you're funny. The beginner classes will teach you what is actually funny." That's a vote of confidence, isn't it, Dr. Susan?

Bret's a comedy lit agent—he should know funny. As it turns out, he doesn't, and I couldn't tell due to my adult onset Asperger's. Maybe I should donate money to NPR during their next pledge drive to thank them for enlightening me. If only I had any money to give. Most of my income from bartending at Duffy's goes toward these therapy sessions, Dr. Susan. Are you telling me that for the last six weeks, I've been throwing my money down the drain?

Dr. Rob said that you came highly recommended. I would have stayed on with him, but he moved his practice to Guam. You aren't planning to move to Guam in the near future, are you, Dr. Susan?

I should have figured something was up with Bret when he didn't laugh at my story about the time I was an exchange student in England. You remember that one, right? I was living with a British family, and I got so drunk that I accidentally used their tea cozy as a maxi pad. It's easily my funniest story, although my homestay family didn't find it too amusing at the time. Okay, so it was a handmade family heirloom, but have you seen what passes for feminine protection in Europe? It's an easy mistake to make.

My relationship with Bret was one of the longest I've ever had. How many of my shorter but equally serious relationships have fallen apart due to my undiagnosed medical conditions? We're talking about years of my life, Dr. Susan. Childbearing years. As Starleigh says, she's not sure I'm believable playing the hot mom, that maybe I should make different choices in scenes. But if I can't play a hot mom onstage, how can I ever be a hot mom in real life?

Here's another missed warning sign: Bret never took me to the movies. I made this connection all by myself, Dr. Susan, and I'm not a "soon-to-be-licensed clinician" like you. Do you see why I am pissed off?

If Bret loved me, then he would have taken me to at least one movie, even a lame one, like *Anchorman 2*. But you never said anything about that connection. And none of my friends or friends of my friends ever said anything either. I think they kept quiet to avoid hurting my feelings, since I put it out on Instagram and Twitter and my YouTube channel just how much I loved Bret. In one particular webisode, I acted out a scene between Bret and me using pantomime: we were having a date at a fancy restaurant. I made up half my face to look like Bret's using eyebrow pencil to mimic his five o'clock shadow, and I absolutely captured his essence, right down to his wandering eye. The pretend date went fabulously—Bret had the lobster thermidor, and I kept the waiters laughing with my spot-on impressions of famous folk singers. I've been told by lots of people that I am a terrific mime. I am apparently a viral hit in France, where mimes are appreciated!

I'm realizing now that my relationship with Bret was obviously discussed behind my back. Sometimes I would notice Tim from my beginners Groundlings class after rehearsal, talking to the other students while pointing at me and laughing.

When I confronted Tim about this, he said he was doing it because he thought I was funny. Then I said that the Second City children's theater almost hired me in 1993 for just that reason. Then Tim said, "No way! I could have seen you—I was five then." Do you see what I'm up against, Dr. Susan?

Dr. Susan, why didn't you say, "Stacy, have you ever thought that maybe people like Tim are laughing at you, not with you?" I might have punched a hole through that Monet poster on your wall, but you're supposed to be honest with me, no matter what. You're supposed to help me navigate these kinds of relationship pitfalls, like getting involved with emotionally unavailable boyfriends. Just because I pay you on the low end of your sliding scale doesn't mean I should receive subpar therapy.

From now on, I'm going to demand that if my friends notice anything odd or off-putting about my boyfriends, they need to tell me immediately because I am suffering from prosopagnosia and can't figure it out myself. Or I might have ADHD. Or a type of non-life-threatening meningitis that has yet to be identified. Do you have an opinion on any of this, Dr. Susan? Because I'm starting to doubt your expertise

I just remembered something else Bret used to do that was suspect: he talked about his ex-wife constantly. How she looked like a cross between Pam Anderson during the *Baywatch* era and that Asian weathergirl on channel 7, that she smelled like lavender, that she picked out the most perfect Caesarstone breakfast bar for their kitchen, and that she was a borderline personality who was taking him to the cleaners in their divorce.

At the time, I thought Bret was unburdening himself to me, his soul mate who should have been the mother of his children, Morgan and Montserrat. In retrospect, he was a major tool like the rest of my exes.

One time when we were together, you know, after doing it, Bret confided in me: he had found out that while they were married, his ex-wife was screwing around with his friend Karl. Contrary to what Starleigh says, I'm a good listener. And I had to listen hard because Bret was going off on a bunch of tangents. Trying to have a heartfelt conversation is hard enough, let alone in a stall in the unisex toilets at Duffy's with drunk Groundlings students pounding on the door, complaining they had to pee. Have you ever seen toilet seats in a bar up close, Dr. Susan?

For the longest time, I thought Bret's ex-wife's name was Johnnie, but after a while, I figured out that when he said, "I miss Johnnie," he was talking about Johnnie Walker Red. These are the little things that I thought endeared me to Bret—knowing his ex-wife wasn't named Johnnie, or making his signature drink before he could even order it, or giving him blow jobs. He seemed so grateful for my attention.

After plugging in some of my other symptoms on WebMD, I think I may also suffer from a disease where I can hear and understand individual words, but I can't make sense of them when they are strung together in a sentence. This explains a lot.

Dr. Susan, maybe that's why I got off the bus at the wrong stop for our first few sessions. I thought El Camino was the model of your car, not the street where your office is located.

When I think about it now, Bret never once asked me about my ex-husband. This may be because I do not have an ex-husband; well, not unless you count the one time I married my cousin on a dare—remind me to tell you about that one, it's a good one—but he never asked me about any of my previous relationships. That's weird, right? Soul mates are supposed to talk about everything. They are supposed to know all about the experimental phase you went through as an exchange student, and all the love affairs that have gone south since you moved to L.A. They are supposed to love you no matter what you've done or whom you've done it to.

Dr. Susan, why didn't you say, "Stacy, has Bret asked about your previous relationships? Does he know who you lost your virginity to?"

It might have prompted me to remember that boyfriends and girlfriends are supposed to have that conversation before they get married, buy a bigger condo, and have twins.

Bret might have been interested to know that I lost my virginity to a certain person who is a fantastic improviser and famous for writing and directing successful comedies such as *Anchorman 2*. Bret might have found himself a lucrative new client thanks to my virginity. I would have been happy to contact this person on Bret's behalf, if this person were still represented by the manager who dumped me two years ago. Or I would have tried for the millionth time to get this person to friend me on Facebook. This person used to be the head writer on *SNL* and could maybe help get me an audition. Or I would have tried harder to get this person to talk to me the few times he showed up at Duffy's. I would have raved about Bret, my fabulous fiancé-to-be on his way up the ladder at WME. I tried sharing this with Bret, but he never wanted to hear about how I lost my virginity. I was sort of disappointed, but I told myself maybe he was one of those guys who didn't like women talking before, during, or after sex.

Bret didn't say much of anything, unless it was about his ex-wife. Maybe it should have been a red flag that after we had sex, Bret would say that having an orgasm helped him block out the image of his friend Karl teabagging his ex-wife whose name is not Johnnie.

The one morning I stayed over at his condo, Bret was leisurely reading *Variety* at his breakfast bar and he didn't even ask me if I wanted coffee. I did ask a bunch of times if he had a coffeemaker and coffee, or if he wanted to go to the Starbucks downstairs, but he kept saying he was on a juice fast. When I screamed I would throw myself off his balcony if I didn't get some caffeine, he just put in his ear buds and ignored me. It's as though he knew about all the other times I had threatened to throw myself off condo balconies and hospital rooftops and high schools and didn't care whether I went through with it.

Dr. Susan, who doesn't need coffee after a night of bartending, drinking too much tequila, doing whip-its in the parking lot, taking the bus to their boyfriend's condo, and waiting hours in the lobby for their boyfriend to show up?

In retrospect, because I was in love and have neurological problems, I let most of Bret's imperfections slide. And also because I have chemical imbalances, but I think I told you about that during our last session. If not, remind me to tell you that story!

Sometimes, I would hang around the lobby of Bret's condo after work and pretend I had stopped by because I was in the neighborhood. If he wasn't there, I'd wait. At first I was chummy with the security guards, but then they got irritated with me after I brought in my sleeping bag and clock radio. They had to know how uncomfortable those couches in the lobby are to sleep on. After I was banned from the lobby, I would sit cross-legged in Bret's parking space in the garage, avoiding the security cameras. When I was down there, a new Lexus sped around the corner, almost running me down. Bret said that he didn't see me, and it was crazy dark down there. I should have gotten suspicious after the fourth time it happened. Dr. Susan, this is what I am so angry about! Why did you not say to me, "Stacy, do you want to spend your life with someone who tries to run you over repeatedly with his car?" If you had put it like that, I might have really heard what you were saying.

Dr. Susan, you should have figured it out. I told you everything. Sure, fifty minutes goes by fast, and it would sometimes seem like I just got started relating all the important details of our relationship, but I think you got the gist. Although you might have taken notes or something. Dr. Rob always took notes during our sessions. At least I think he did. One time I caught him doodling.

Okay, back to me. I ran into Bret recently. I served this girl, her name is Gina or Tina something—I met her through my Groundlings friends. She's in the intermediate class, so I tried to impress her with my tea cozy story, until she excused herself to make a phone call. Twenty-five minutes later, I saw her and Bret snogging right in front of the bar.

Bret did not see me but I definitely saw him. All I could do was look down at Gina or Tina's sparkly cheapo heels. If only Bret had looked at her feet, then he would have noticed she needed a pedicure big-time. Toenails say a lot about a person, Dr. Susan. I've learned that lesson the hard way.

It's a terrible realization, but Bret would rather make out with a woman with disgusting chipped toenails than get married, buy a bigger condo, and have babies with me.

While we were seriously dating, Bret never asked me about birth control, especially after I reassured him that I was on the Pill. Okay, I sometimes forgot to take my birth control pills. It's not like I did it on purpose. I read somewhere on WebMD that memory lapse can be another symptom of meningitis.

But Bret knew how much I wanted to have kids. Any time we went anywhere together, like his parking garage in the alley behind Duffy's, I would ooh and aah over any babies we might see, and if we didn't see any babies, I did the same thing with dogs. Dogs are basically stand-ins for babies, everyone knows that. You have a dog, Dr. Susan, don't you? A French poodle? Or was that Dr. Rob's dog? I hope that dog is living it up in Guam.

So when I told him that I had possibly missed my period, I thought he would have been happy. But he just turned kind of green. I told Bret it didn't matter that I would be the oldest hot mom on the playground; I said our child would be quirky with me as its mother and great at being an agent with him as its father. Although him being a great agent is up for debate since he apparently can't tell what's funny or not. Maybe he's on the spectrum too!

I told him that I wasn't completely sure just yet because the pregnancy test I took from CVS was inconclusive, but that I had had a very realistic dream I was pregnant. I should have known something was up when he asked me, "How are pregnancy tests inconclusive? Aren't they either positive or negative?" If he had cared about me, he would have taken me at my word, not made me buy another test and take it in front of him. I still think that the minus sign is going to ultimately turn into a plus sign. Sometimes it takes time for the hormones to show up in one's bloodstream.

I should have known something was up when I texted him Morgan and Montserrat as possible baby names and he never texted back. I should have known that every time I called Bret at work, his assistant refused to put me through, and after a while, started hanging up on me. And when I finally ran into Bret, he was Frenching gross-toed Gina or Tina.

I told you about how much I wanted to have a baby, Dr. Susan, remember? Couldn't you have suggested to me gently that Bret might not be the right guy to father Morgan and Montserrat?

What's tragic about this situation is that I can't raise a baby by myself, Dr. Susan. Not since all these neurological issues have come to light. What if I mistook the baby for the garbage and threw it out accidentally? Or left it on the bus because I thought it was a newspaper? Given my spectrum disorder, it could happen.

On the bus ride over here, I looked out the window and up Hollywood Boulevard, and I saw a beautiful woman walking on the sidewalk. She was wearing short shorts, and her tanned legs looked gorgeous in a pair of expensive-looking high heels. I could imagine her beautifully pedicured toenails. She looked like a woman with a purpose, with direction. At that moment, I believed in my heart that I could be someone just like her, if only I wasn't someone just like me. As the bus drove by, I don't know what came over me. I yelled out the window, "Fuck yourself, bitch!" The woman looked surprised and her face crumpled, as though she was about to cry. I started to feel guilty, but then she looked right at me and spit on the ground and grabbed her crotch. It was only then I realized she wasn't a woman at all.

I know our time is up, Dr. Susan, but where does this leave me? What about Morgan and Montserrat? And why do you keep looking at me like that? Like Starleigh asks during improv class, "Where's the life behind your eyes?"

The Old Gang

I AM LOOKING OVER THE CRACKERS IN THE cracker aisle at Ralphs when I recognize Jeff Taich. I love this Ralphs because it has an entire aisle dedicated to crackers. At the other Ralphs east of Laurel Canyon, there is a combination "cookie/cracker" aisle. It's not nearly enough variety of either crackers or cookies. I complained once to the store manager, and he just looked at me and my grocery bags full of wine and Triscuits until I got self-conscious and slunk out the automatic doors.

It's been my experience that when your dinner consists of two bottles of cheap red wine, Triscuits eaten at key points throughout the evening cushion the blow to your soft tissues. I may not have learned that much in my life, but in the category of foods to eat while getting shitfaced, I'm an expert.

I catch a glimpse of a bony profile reaching for a jumbo box of Ritz Crackers and immediately the name "Jeff Taich" pops into my head. Even though I pretend to be engrossed in cracker packaging, I see Jeff Taich do a double take once he notices me. His neck, craned at an angle from looking at all the Ritz varietals, sticks out even more awkwardly as he sizes me up.

I haven't seen Jeff Taich in years, so I'm surprised I recognize him. Lately I have trouble remembering names, but I can't be too impressed with myself, because given our unfortunate history, Jeff Taich qualifies as an exception. I'm not all that worried because I'm too young for the memory to go just yet. Forty-five would have been elderly back in the Middle Ages, but here in the twenty-first century, I'm still practically an adolescent. I'm confident that I have time left to accomplish something.

After a few minutes of us glancing back and forth, the tension gets the best of me. I suppose I could have pretended that I didn't recognize Jeff Taich's older, bonier, definitely uglier face, and beat it out of the cracker aisle, but it felt like a cop-out. I don't usually like confrontation, but once in a while, I feel the need to punch first. It's not my best attribute.

"Hey, Jeff," I say.

Jeff Taich looks up as though the chickenshit hadn't noticed me. People in L.A. feign surprise like that all the time—*Oh, I was totally lost in my own head, thinking of a million things, like calculating when I would have time to update Facebook, or contemplating which Ralphs has the better cracker aisle.* What a pussy.

"Hey, Mark," Jeff Taich says, but the look in his eyes says, *Oh shit.*

I wouldn't say that Jeff Taich and I were ever friends. Back in the early 1990s, when we both lived in Chicago, we ran with O'Hanlon's crowd. Who remembers how Jeff Taich fell in with the group? But I met O'Hanlon at work. I had started temping at a commercial real estate company in the Loop after college. O'Hanlon worked in the mailroom, which was worse than my job making copies and doing Starbucks runs for puffy agents, guys whom you would see outside the building smoking during a heat wave, sweating straight through their navy suits. Because we were both low men on the corporate totem pole, O'Hanlon often got pulled in to help me with useless administrative projects.

When I first met O'Hanlon, he was skinny, maybe 135 pounds. He wasn't tall, but he carried himself as though he were Michael Jordan, if Michael Jordan was a WASPy kid from Kenilworth. He had a kind of gleam in his eye that, upon first inspection, one might classify as mischievous, but those of us who hung out with him on a regular basis knew the truth: at his core, O'Hanlon was a salesman. He could use his charms to coerce anyone to do anything. O'Hanlon Senior worked at the firm and had secured the mailroom job for his youngest son. He was hell-bent on seeing O'Hanlon Junior make it in the business.

"You gotta pay your dues," O'Hanlon's dad said when he visited him in the mailroom. "Prove yourself first. No guts, no glory." O'Hanlon's dad had a big Irish face and pale eyebrows, and bore absolutely no resemblance to his son. O'Hanlon made a jerk-off motion with his hand after his father left.

"That guy's a douchebag," he said with a straight face.

"I can see that," I said.

"Your dad must be like a double douchebag—look at you," he said.

My dad had told me shortly after graduation that if I didn't start creating some kind of a future for myself, he'd kick me out of the upstairs unit of our family two-flat.

"Your job might be crappy, but it keeps you off the streets," he said. As if he'd ever let me roam the mean streets anyway, despite threatening to oust me from the premises. After my mom died, I think he liked having someone else around, even though by the time I moved to California, we had little to say to each other. When I think about it now, I cringe at how much money he was wasting letting me stay there for free. He could've made a killing renting that apartment to some yuppie-in-training whose wet dream was to live in Lincoln Park.

"I worry about the fate of this country with slackers like you eventually running things," Dad said. He had a patriotic streak that could be irritating.

O'Hanlon and I were the youngest and by far the most carefree people working at the firm. Things like cholesterol numbers and mutual funds—big topics of conversation among our bleary coworkers—might as well have been quantum physics to us. We were much more interested in extracurricular activities.

O'Hanlon and I smoked a lot of weed, listened to Nirvana, and loved *This Is Spinal Tap*. Most of all, we hated working for The Man. Oh, how we hated it! We despised having to collate documents, lining up the paper clips perfectly on the left-hand margins so that our bitch of a boss wouldn't scream. We couldn't have cared less about our job performance. Sometimes, in the mornings after a late night, I would catch O'Hanlon asleep in the mailroom, lying in a cart of undelivered mail. We usually passed the eight hours of workday boredom by quoting our favorite lines from *Airplane!*

"Son, ever seen a grown man naked?" O'Hanlon would ask me, apropos of nothing. It never failed to crack me up.

"Cubs-Angels game?" O'Hanlon said on a Thursday morning in the spring. "Bleacher seats at noon?" He dug into the cheese Danish his mom packed him for breakfast. He still lived at home, but I never gave him shit about his mommy sending him off to work with both breakfast and lunch lovingly packed in his messenger bag. It's because I knew somehow he would turn it on me—how I was a loser because I had to spend my own money on meals.

"Your mother doesn't love you," O'Hanlon would often say. "And she's dead. Boohoo." Not much was off-limits to O'Hanlon, including my dead mother. She would have liked him, though she would have seen through his bravado.

I gestured toward my boss's office. "Can't," I said.

O'Hanlon would never take no for an answer. Must have been due to the fact that he was the youngest of eight brothers and sisters.

"Guess you really like this job," O'Hanlon started in. "You're a real company man."

That's all it took. I told my boss that I couldn't work that afternoon because I was having a diarrhea attack that came on suddenly.

"Thanks for the visual," she said. "You are a colossal waste of time."

I backed out of her office, hands jammed in my pockets, both of my middle fingers up. Then O'Hanlon patted me on the back as we got into the elevator.

"You make me proud, son," he said.

O'Hanlon's group consisted of rotating members, depending on the activity or who was available. There was Jeff Taich. Also Jill somebody, a tomboy type from Iowa. A guy O'Hanlon referred to as "Crazy Mike from the South Side." I never asked what Crazy Mike's real name was, not that it mattered. There were others on the O'Hanlon periphery: guys he met in the cheap seats at Cubs games, two girls he tried to pick up on the brown line, even an entire intramural softball team he played against the summer before. O'Hanlon liked being the ringleader, and he was damn good at it. I've subsequently met other people like O'Hanlon, but they never seem as impressive to me as he did. They seem pathetic in their need to be popular. I never felt that way about O'Hanlon. Maybe I didn't know any better.

I am staring at Jeff Taich like an idiot in the cracker aisle and he's staring back at me.

"I didn't know you moved out here," I say finally.

"Yeah," Jeff says, "about five years ago. For a job."

I confess that I never had any idea what Jeff Taich did for a living. He could be a coal miner for all I know. When we were hanging out back then, none of us ever talked about anything work related. We just drank a ton of beer and smoked a lot of weed, and magically, we all had the important things in common. We were brothers and sisters, wrestling our lives out of the brown ice of the city. Some of us were more successful at it than others.

Jeff Taich looks well fed and well dressed. He's wearing wingtips in the grocery store for chrissakes. Who wears wingtips anymore? Especially in L.A.?

You look like my father circa 1979 is what I want to say, but instead I say, "You keep in touch with anyone from Chicago?"

Why I asked that, I have no idea. I don't care if Jeff Taich keeps in touch with anyone from Chicago. Jeff Taich shifts his weight from one khaki-clad leg to another.

"Not really," he says. "O'Hanlon's brother Timmy found me on LinkedIn, but that's about it. He's a tax attorney, like me."

Of course, I think.

Back in the day, O'Hanlon talked most of us into forming a coed beach volleyball team in the summer, even though the games were usually called due to rain or lack of female members. He coerced us into watching old movies on Sunday nights at the Brew and View at the Vic, and forced us to brave the humidity and the crowds for the free concerts in Grant Park. I went along because he was fun to be around. No offense to O'Hanlon's organizational talents, but he wrangled us mostly as an excuse to party as much as possible. I can say in all honesty that I no longer enjoy drinking in large groups out in public. My taste for that kind of thing has ebbed away. I prefer the privacy of my own apartment, where I can sit on my couch, watch *The Next Food Network Star* on TiVo, drink my dinner, and leisurely pass out. I don't need the likes of Jeff Taich laughing at my slurred speech, or commenting on how inexpertly I was hitting on the chunky but semi-hot blond girl sitting at the next table at the Cubby Bear.

"Have you ever gotten any poontang?" O'Hanlon would ask after he had goaded me into chatting up yet another drunk girl in a baseball hat at any given North Side bar. "Have you gone through puberty yet? Have you ever seen a gladiator movie?"

"Screw you," I'd say, after cracking up at the *Airplane!* reference.

"I haven't thought about Timmy in years. What was he, like two years older than O'Hanlon?" I say to Jeff Taich. I move my cart out of the way for other shoppers looking for crackers.

"I guess he's still in Chicago," Jeff Taich says. "The O'Hanlons will never leave that city. Too much there for them. Me, I moved to St. Louis in '97 for law school. Haven't been back to Chi-town since, except for the ten-year memorial. I felt like I owed it to O'Hanlon's family."

I cringe—the few times I ever got an e-mail about a memorial for O'Hanlon, I deleted the correspondence unread. Something unyielding in the pit of my stomach made me do it. I don't have the balls to revisit the past, even though it would maybe be the right thing to do. I don't have the balls for a lot of things anymore. I guess that's one of the gifts that age offers up—an understanding of the world as a ruthless place devoid of mercy, and yet I still manage to get up for work the next day. Besides, the last person O'Hanlon's family would want to see is me. I'm no tax attorney, but even I know better than that.

One Tuesday night, in the middle of January, O'Hanlon talked Jeff Taich and me into drinking at some dive on Lincoln Avenue. We were the only people apparently stupid enough to leave our warm apartments. Hardly anyone was at the bar that night; even the alcoholic regulars had called it quits early. Dirty snow from a storm weeks earlier that had turned to ice covered the curbs, the weather too cold for it to melt. This is the city I remember most vividly: the gray skies, the frigid air. Winter settling in for a good, long chat; a heaviness that wouldn't lift until maybe the middle of April, if you were lucky. That night, we started with pitchers of Old Style and a friendly game of quarters. At a certain point, we blew off the game and switched to Jäger shots.

"By opening day," O'Hanlon said, "we need to get you laid. It's a tough job, but someone has to do it." I remember Jeff Taich laughing. I realize now, seeing Jeff Taich again in the flesh, that I can't remember much else about him except his lame laugh. He was boring as shit. No wonder he became a tax attorney.

"Never heard that one before," I said, downing my shot.

There was no way I could explain my dry spell to O'Hanlon. He wasn't a person with patience for complicated scenarios. I refused to give it much thought myself, until later. All I knew at the time was that it felt like a black hole, the consequences of fucking; who to fuck and where to fuck them, and the delicious jolt of desire when I got that look, the *follow me into the alley and fuck me* look. How could I explain to O'Hanlon the more I followed my dick, or my heart, or whatever it was, into the dark bars and the bathhouses, the more urgent the wanting became. In truth, I could scarcely think of anything else. Often, I would feel like bursting into tears. How could I tell O'Hanlon that more times than I was able to count, I went in search of someone thin and dark and willing, someone who reminded me of him, after I had called it a night with the old gang? How could I expect him to understand?

In my moments of clarity, which were few and far between in those days, the cons always outweighed the pros of ever coming clean.

"Make a pro/con list when you're trying to make a decision," my dad said. "It's easy once you put those brain cells to work, if you have any left."

I am positive that my dad did not have this kind of situation in mind when he recommended it to me. I don't think he would have wanted to know that his only son was cruising Boystown bars on a school night.

"You're a pussy," Jeff Taich said. "Just be a man and find some ass. Any ass is better than no ass." He and O'Hanlon clinked glasses and downed their shots.

"Fuck you both," I said. The bar had started to spin.

"Do you like it out here?" I ask Jeff Taich. I couldn't care less what he liked, but I was trying to ease out of the conversation as nonchalantly as possible.

"Sure, what's not to like? The weather's great, not like Chicago."

No duh, I thought.

"Still, there's a lot I miss about the Midwest. We had ourselves some fun. Guess we're getting old now."

"Not so old," I say hopefully.

Jeff Taich gives me a condescending look. "Oh, we're old all right. Even O'Hanlon would have turned forty a few years ago. He was a hell of a guy. Can't find too many people like that anymore. He just had charisma I guess," Jeff Taich says.

Too bad we ruined that for him, I want to say, but I shrug instead.

"I knew it was time to grow up after all that went down," he says.

I didn't think I would panic, here in my Ralphs, in my cracker aisle, but I feel my heart starting to race. Shoppers are making their way around Jeff Taich and me, giving us looks for blocking the aisle. I hope to recognize one of them, desperate for a way out of this conversation. I am sweating through my shirt, stuck here talking to Jeff Taich, a hell of my own making. If O'Hanlon were here, he would laugh.

Surely you can find a reason to stop talking to this prick, he'd say.

I can, but stop calling me Shirley.

After a few more Jäger shots, it was almost midnight. We rolled out of the bar. Even though I was drunk, I remember being hit in the face with a blast of lake effect air, a sinus cavity freezer of a night if there ever was one. We tried to find a cab, but no one was out in the cold on a weeknight.

"The shit-brown line it is," O'Hanlon said.

O'Hanlon was the first to jump the turnstile at the Montrose el station. It wasn't a big deal since the station was deserted and the person taking tickets was asleep in his chair. Jeff Taich and O'Hanlon were cackling about something in front of me as they weaved across the platform. I suspected they were attacking my masculinity for the umpteenth time that evening. I started to get nauseated. *Do they know?* I asked myself drunkenly. *Does O'Hanlon know?* Had they seen me, or heard something from someone else? Or had they always known? O'Hanlon strutted, doing his best Mick Jagger.

"He can't get no, no satisfaction," he sang. Jeff Taich fell over laughing. The bile rose in my throat.

"Maybe he wants dick," Jeff Taich said. "O'Hanlon, you better watch your ass when you bend over, down there in the mailroom with this guy."

The next thing I knew, my fist made contact with Jeff Taich's jaw. He ended up flat on the el platform before hopping up and charging at me in an adrenaline-fueled rage. At this point, I remember being dimly aware of red lights in the distance, before O'Hanlon tried to get in the middle of us.

"Break it up," he said in his best Little League referee voice, practiced over years of working for the Wilmette Park District.

Jeff Taich and I were still going at it, fists flailing but making little contact.

"I said, break it up!" O'Hanlon pulled my arm hard till I heard a snap and felt a flash of pain.

"Fuck you!" I screamed, and shoved against Jeff Taich hard. We both hit O'Hanlon full on before smashing ourselves onto the concrete platform. My arm throbbed as I struggled to get to my feet. O'Hanlon fell closer to the edge of the tracks. He stood up and tried to steady himself, but instead he tipped, almost gracefully, over the side. I ran to the edge and peered down, just in time to see O'Hanlon's surprised face. He was laughing, and then I can't remember anything except the roar of the train as it entered the station.

"I guess I'll be seeing you in the neighborhood," Jeff Taich says. He puts out his hand, which I shake halfheartedly.

"Yeah," I say.

Jeff Taich notices the wine bottles carefully stacked in my cart.

"It's funny, after the accident, I stopped drinking, cold turkey. Just like that," Jeff Taich says. "I was so drunk that night, I couldn't remember what happened, even at the police station. We were all just joking around. Then I was lying on the platform. And then there was screaming.

That was me screaming, I want to say. An older woman passing by listens in and then looks suspiciously at us before picking up a box of water crackers and walking away.

"Guy never had a chance, poor drunk bastard," Jeff Taich says, slapping me on the back with his jumbo box of Ritzes, maybe as some kind of show of solidarity.

I'd like to fly over the front of my cart and knock out all of Jeff Taich's permanently whitened teeth. O'Hanlon. The poor drunk bastard. Too bad he ever met the likes of us.

"Find me on LinkedIn," Jeff Taich says, putting the box of Ritzes under his arm as he walks off. I watch him greet a woman at the end of the aisle. She's holding the hand of a kid of about five. Looking at them, I wonder what O'Hanlon would be doing if he were alive today. He'd likely still be stuck in Chicago. He'd have a good but boring sales job that he'd be great at, a wife, a family. He'd have moved back to the suburbs for the better public schools and to be closer to his aging parents. He probably would have put on some weight, like we all have. His life would have become about his mortgage, parent-teacher conferences, running errands, life insurance—it would have no longer been his own. Or maybe he would be working twelve-hour shifts supporting computer software like me, and then come home to no one in particular. Like me, maybe in the middle of the night when he's supposed to be sleeping, he would find himself wondering whether anyone in the world cares that he is alive. Perhaps it's for the best O'Hanlon never had to come to the realization that after a while, we all stop trying, just like those guys at the firm we snickered at. Maybe he's lucky his life ended before everything went to shit.

I put the box of Triscuits in my cart and decide that another trip to the wine aisle is definitely in order. Or maybe a bottle of vodka would be best of all, just to take the sting off the day. Maybe if I'm lucky, O'Hanlon's laughing face won't be the last thing I see tonight before I close my eyes. Maybe tonight I won't dream of him playing one of the half-drunk pranks he used to play on me all the time.

Looks like I picked the wrong week to quit sniffing glue, O'Hanlon says, before shoving me, maybe just a little bit harder than usual, toward the platform edge.

Kevin Kramer Starts on Monday

KEVIN KRAMER STARTS HIS NEW JOB ON MONDAY. The executive team counts down the minutes to his arrival. The executive team is made up of four white men, one woman, and one man who claims to be a "Pacific Islander" on tax forms, but everyone knows he's Armenian.

Kevin Kramer is exactly what the products profit center needs in a senior vice president. He was groomed in corporate. According to Kevin Kramer's impressive résumé, he worked previously for Procter and Gamble, Hewlett-Packard, and Mrs. Fields. According to the transcripts from his breakfast interviews, Kevin Kramer lives and breathes corporate.

Kevin Kramer speaks in a low baritone, softly but with authority. He talks about concepts like "tonnage" and "low-hanging fruit." Even though 85 percent of the executives surveyed had no idea what Kevin Kramer was talking about, 100 percent of them fell in love with Kevin Kramer from his first interview.

Kevin Kramer is a pro. He always maintains eye contact. His handshake is firm, but not too firm. His hands are supple and moisture-free. One executive, after shaking Kevin Kramer's hand, thought his fingers felt a bit rough. It turned out that Kevin Kramer played bass for years with his band, the Butt Gerbils. When they couldn't get any gigs, they changed their name to Punkster. That executive later fantasized about Kevin Kramer playing "Stairway to Heaven" onstage with Robert Plant. She thought about Kevin Kramer touching her with his rough, bass-hardened fingertips, and she came harder than she had in months.

Kevin Kramer says, "Leaders aren't afraid to hurt people's feelings in the best interests of the company. Leaders have no problems dispensing justice swiftly. Leaders never lose sleep at night. I sleep like a baby." This is why Kevin Kramer starts on Monday.

The executive team cheers when they see Kevin Kramer drive his navy-blue BMW into the parking lot Monday morning. One executive says, "Let the hammer fall. Godspeed."

This executive never washes his hands after visiting the men's room. He also refuses to say thank you when someone holds the door to the patio open for him, unless that person is another executive or that sexy Indian girl in software.

When Kevin Kramer starts on Monday, he parks in his own parking space, with his name in bold on a placard. No one else in the company has ever had their own personally designated parking space, not even the CEO. Eighty percent of employees surveyed complained about the lack of parking. Kevin Kramer realizes that many in the company will be angered by this change to the parking space policy.

But Kevin Kramer refused to take the position of senior vice president unless he could be assured of his own parking space, and the executives agreed to his demand, provided that they too would receive their own parking spaces. The executives also tabled the plan to build a new parking garage for everyone else until 2020.

On Monday, HR sends out an e-mail explaining the new parking space policy. So as not to single out Kevin Kramer, the e-mail mentions the others who are important enough to get their own spaces. One executive says, "It's about fucking time!"

This executive used the word "fuck" as much as possible, because he liked to think of himself as Tony Soprano, if Tony Soprano had been born in St. Louis and became a CPA.

Kevin Kramer has been hired to put new corporate efficiencies into place. Kevin Kramer makes these efficiencies up during meetings. He does his best work under pressure.

Kevin Kramer starts on Monday because the executives decided the company needed a paradigm shift. The CEO Jon Goldfarb had become too involved with everyday operations. He was a nice guy but an egghead. He was socially awkward with clients at hockey games and other events that were supposed to be fun, not painful.

According to a survey, 72 percent of clients characterized Jon Goldfarb as "annoying." One client wrote on the comment section of the survey, "Can someone please teach Jon Goldfarb the fundamentals of baseball so he can stop quoting actuarial tables when the bases are loaded in the bottom of the ninth?"

The executives also decided that Jon Goldfarb was too big of a softie to get rid of dead weight, and as a result, unproductive employees had been hanging on to their jobs for years. These employees did zero work while gobbling up health benefits and overtime and accumulated paid time off. The executives hoped that the new senior vice president would fire the employees doing their jobs poorly. The executives also wanted the senior vice president to bring a hipper vibe to the company, making it more "relevant" and "twenty-first century," which 56 percent of surveyed clients indicated were desirable traits for their payroll company to have.

Kevin Kramer is a tough negotiator. He told Jon Goldfarb during his breakfast interview, "Your company is in the toilet. The competition wants to bury you, and while you waver trying to make a decision, they will hire me. And then I will bury you."

Jon Goldfarb sipped his coffee and pushed his eggs around his plate. He personally found Kevin Kramer to be kind of an asshole, but he had read the survey that indicated 100 percent of the executives believed he was "the guy," so he offered him the job. This is why Kevin Kramer gets whatever he desires.

Kevin Kramer's office is new. Architects were hired to build his new office out of a corner office and a neighboring file room. The burliest members of the facilities department were offered overtime to spend a weekend moving the files out of the file room. When a few smaller employees complained that they were being discriminated against due to their size, HR arranged for everyone in facilities to receive Subway coupons. That shut everyone up.

Kevin Kramer is introduced around the products profit center on Monday morning. He meets Judy, a hefty woman with white hair who is in charge of user acceptance testing. Judy has been an employee at the company for twenty years. Her passion is not user acceptance testing, but "Judy's Corner," a column in the company newsletter. "Judy's Corner" is filled with employee anecdotes and upbeat sayings that allude to Jesus Christ.

It is company policy that all religions are tolerated, even religions that 79 percent of surveyed employees considered "weird." Because of this and because of all the new employees in software development recently outsourced from a company in India, Judy has been told to steer clear of Jesus in her column. She sometimes reprints *Family Circus* cartoons when she's out of ideas.

Kevin Kramer says, "It's a pleasure to meet the famous Judy." He was given the latest issue of the newsletter at his breakfast interview. He read it while taking a dump that Monday morning at home.

Judy beams, saying, "Kevin, I want to include a personal story from you for the 'Corner' this month," to which Kevin Kramer replies, "I'd be happy to." But later that Monday, Judy receives an e-mail from HR, telling her that unless she takes the early retirement package offered her, she risks losing all her benefits. By the end of the day, she is gone.

Forty-seven percent of employees surveyed thought the company newsletter was "pointless." Thirty-six percent thought it was "heartwarming," "a great way to stay abreast of employee happenings," and "the only way to find out if any retired employees had died."

The executive team had plans to revamp the newsletter into an interactive website, but they never got to that item on the agenda during their offsite planning session at the Beverly Hills Hotel.

Getting rid of Judy is just another reason the executives are happy to see Kevin Kramer in his new corner office, standing on his eight-hundred-dollar Aeron chair.

After Kevin Kramer starts on Monday, the old guard starts to get nervous. The old guard are those employees who, when surveyed, thought it was okay to wear their pajamas to work. Some of the new guard will also be nervous, but only those who had gotten comfortable wearing shower shoes to work. The new guard figures that the old guard will have to go first, before Kevin Kramer sets his sights on them. But Kevin Kramer is unpredictable. For example, while he did away with the company newsletter, he inexplicably kept the interdepartmental potlucks going for a time. He even contributed a crockpot of chili that he claimed came from a family recipe.

If any of the employees who chowed down on Kevin Kramer's chili thought it tasted off, or maybe that it smelled like dog food, they will never tell each other, let alone Kevin Kramer. No one will ever tell Kevin Kramer the truth, and no one knows this better than Kevin Kramer himself.

For a few months, Kevin Kramer does little work. He observes the products profit center's workflow. He attends meetings but says nothing. He spends most of the time looking out his office window, watching the employees smoke in the courtyard or slurp their 7-Eleven Slurpees.

He wanders the floor of the call center, and, hiding behind the potted ficus trees, listens to the representatives answer client calls. He refuses invitations to lunch from other executives, which makes them squirm. He spends hours in the break room, buying up all the strawberry Pop-Tarts.

He chats with Doc, the security guard, about Doc's years in the Marine Corps. Kevin Kramer doesn't understand a word of what Doc says, because no one understands a word of what Doc says. In that regard, Kevin Kramer is no different from anyone else in the company.

Finally, Kevin Kramer devises a plan. He doesn't create a spreadsheet or a PowerPoint presentation. He doesn't tell Jon Goldfarb, even though Jon Goldfarb has been asking for a status report for weeks. This type of behavior solidifies Jon Goldfarb's opinion that Kevin Kramer is a big douchebag. But Kevin Kramer's survey numbers have been rising every week since he started, so Jon Goldfarb keeps his mouth shut.

At this point, Kevin Kramer hires an assistant. It is Kevin Kramer's practice to watch his workload pile up until it appears he will never be able to get on track. Then he hires an assistant whom he has already chosen in his mind. Kevin Kramer calls Debi Baker in human resources to let her know whom he has decided on.

"Kevin, the way it works around here is that HR hires all new employees. We need to interview candidates and see résumés," Debi says.

"Debi, you have intimate knowledge of my new assistant, because you will be my new assistant," Kevin Kramer says.

Debi pauses and finally says, "Kevin, I'm not an assistant; I've been in human resources for twenty-five years, so . . ."

"Do you accept your new position as my assistant, or will you leave the company of your own volition?" Kevin Kramer says, munching on a Twizzler.

Debi says nothing.

Kevin Kramer waits on the line, listening to Debi wheeze. Debi mentioned during Kevin Kramer's employee orientation that she has terrible asthma that acts up when she's stressed out. Asthma was the only thing Debi talked about during the new-employee orientation. She told the new employees, "Just read the handbook to learn about your benefits. It's the standard crap you've seen a thousand times."

"Okay," she says finally. Then she hangs up.

Kevin Kramer estimates that Debi will last five weeks as his assistant. Kevin Kramer is always right about these things. As he suspects, she is a terrible assistant. Kevin enjoys asking her to stay late to research special paint that can turn his office walls into giant white boards. He makes Debi come in at six in the morning to answer support calls from international clients. He offers her services to whatever area of the products profit center is short-staffed during the workday, and then asks her to do his work after six or on weekends.

Kevin Kramer listens to Debi wheeze in her cubicle, listens to her weep, until HR informs him that she has gone out on stress leave. Then he replaces her with Jenna, a support representative from the call center. Jenna seems eager to move up in the company. She has a golden tan and wears short skirts. Kevin Kramer noticed her right away during one of his secret excursions to the call center, her headset slightly askew on her head due to a clump of hair extensions.

Kevin Kramer has a thin, pretty wife and two adorable children with wide-set eyes just like him. But like any executive groomed in corporate, he does not mind a little eye candy around the office. He does not mind an office flirtation and, if the situation calls for it, a quickie on his antique desk.

The first quarterly meeting where Kevin Kramer is in attendance is a happening. He is treated like a rock star. The executives surround him, hoping to get into his good graces by complimenting his Brooks Brothers shirt. Most lower-tier employees are too shy to approach him, but a few brave or stupid ones try unsuccessfully to chat him up before one of the executives shoos them away. Jenna is one of the few who is allowed to approach Kevin Kramer at the meeting.

Forty-eight percent of employees surveyed called the quarterly meetings "thinly veiled attempts to spin lousy performance numbers into gold." One person commented, "One would find more truth in a North Korean radio broadcast." Twenty-four percent wrote that they "wished there were more variety in the breakfast offerings, including some gluten-free options."

Kevin Kramer samples the muffins and the low-pulp orange juice, and sits in the front row. Many significant issues are discussed during the meeting, such as client survey results and the company's plan to rearrange the lobby furniture. Kevin Kramer's mind wanders to Jenna's firm ass. He doesn't pay attention in the meeting, because once his plan is implemented, all client survey results will be shredded. Also, to increase sagging revenues, the lobby will be rented out to an H&R Block franchise, and it will bring in its own furniture.

One executive presenting at the meeting says, "Our company employs some of the smartest people I've ever known. And we've just gotten ten IQ points smarter with the addition of Kevin Kramer!"

Everyone applauds, and Kevin Kramer is jolted out of his reverie. He realizes that people are clapping for him. He stands up and waves. Afterward, every other executive makes a point to say how smart everyone in the products profit center is, even though 100 percent of the executives surveyed indicated that "trained chimps could do a better job than most of the employees."

Kevin Kramer was born in Skokie, Illinois, to educator parents. Kevin's mother remembers Kevin helping her load the dishwasher every night after dinner. Kevin's father remembers that Kevin had an avid interest in marine biology when he was a kid.

Kevin Kramer was a decent student, but did not distinguish himself in any way. He applied to the University of Michigan and Northwestern and was rejected by both.

After two semesters at Oakton Community College, he was able to transfer to the University of Illinois at Urbana-Champaign, where he dropped out after his junior year. Kevin's parents, when surveyed, cited that he "seemed to lag socially behind the other students."

Kevin Kramer's résumé lists his alma maters as Northwestern University for undergrad and the University of Michigan for his MBA.

Kevin Kramer puts his efficiencies into place slowly. Initially, every other garbage can disappears from the products profit center floor. Employees are told that they must share garbage cans with their neighbors. A few grumble, but most accept the change without incident.

Then employees realize the fluorescent overhead lights seem dimmer than they used to be. Under Kevin Kramer's cost-cutting plan, every other lightbulb is taken out of the fixtures. Some employees with astigmatism complain, and a few get doctors' notes and go out on stress leave.

When Kevin Kramer started working in the corporate world years ago, he was paunchy and always seemed to be sweating. But after carefully studying the executives he worked under, Kevin Kramer wised up. He hired a personal trainer and got his teeth whitened and started smiling more, so that his sweatiness seemed less gross. It's gotten to the point now where no one even notices the sweat circles under the armpits of Kevin Kramer's faintly checkered Brooks Brothers shirts. People instead are fixated on his poker face, looking for signs. Since a meeting during second quarter that 45 percent of the attendees found "worthwhile, for once," only to learn two hours later that they had all been terminated, no one knows what to make of anything that Kevin Kramer says. They only know to fear him, which is exactly what Kevin Kramer depends on.

Kevin Kramer demands information on a constant basis. He makes managers compile data on customer complaints into five spreadsheets separated out by product and complaint, only to demand the same information in a graph format and also as a PowerPoint. He halts all development of software, telling the executives, "We're not in the business of software development; we're in the business of people development." He contracts with an expensive life coach to help oversee the department, and then fires her after a week.

Kevin Kramer personally writes phone scripts for the call center representatives to use when speaking to clients. The scripts begin, "Thank you for calling Entertainment Solutions. We're people who get it!" He demands that managers write up any representative who does not stick to the script. He fires several representatives who, while sticking to the script, do not comply with his new "no shower shoes at work" edict.

Kevin Kramer demands new budgets from each department that must be 30 percent lower than the old budgets. Kevin Kramer will never look at all the information painstakingly collected and delivered to him on schedule. He asks Jenna to shred every document on his desk. He enjoys watching Jenna, wearing a fitted pantsuit, bending over the shredder, feeding in each piece of paper one by one.

Kevin takes Jenna to lunch for her performance review. During the meal, Jenna peppers him with questions:

"So how did you get started in business?" she asks. "What advice can you give to a young go-getter like me?"

Kevin Kramer orders a glass of Zinfandel. He tells Jenna that he got his first job at a commercial real estate company in downtown Chicago. He started watching the executives, and figured out quickly it was the way he wanted his career path to go. He neglects to tell Jenna that most of the executives he studied did nothing except take meetings, go to lunches, and play golf. After a while, Kevin Kramer began to sell a lot of commercial real estate to start-up companies—companies that had no real product but lots of money due to the dot-com boom. Kevin Kramer was savvy enough to know that he needed to get out quickly if he wanted to make a huge profit.

After a few more glasses of wine, Kevin Kramer tells Jenna that he lived with his parents for a long time, into his late twenties, because he was saving his money. He never wanted to have a starter home, or car, or wife. Kevin Kramer wanted only the best for himself, so he waited, patiently, honing his business acumen. Even though Kevin Kramer is a little drunk, he knew better than to tell Jenna that he owed much of his success in business to teeth-whitening treatments.

After several hours, Jenna tells Kevin that she has to go home to feed her cat.

"I'll let you drive back to the office," he says, throwing her the keys to his Beemer.

Kevin Kramer wants to hold Jenna's hand while she drives, but he can't figure out the best way to position himself.

"Thank you for lunch," Jenna says after pulling into his space. "It was neat hearing all your stories." Then she hops out before Kevin Kramer can attempt to kiss her.

Kevin realizes that he didn't give Jenna any feedback on her job performance. When he is surveyed, he calls her "a flawless worker" and says that she makes "everything seem effortless."

Kevin Kramer sends out an e-mail to everyone in the products profit center, explaining that for the financial health of the company, the department is to be reorganized. He makes everyone change cubicles twice in a two-week period, citing "productivity principles" and "agile business units." He dismantles the break room and turns it into a storage area, saying, "A new and improved Zen break room will be built by fourth quarter, or whenever the funds become available." He merges the software developers with the IT department, claiming, "They all do the same thing anyway."

Kevin Kramer has facilities change the toilet paper in the restrooms to cheaper one-ply sheets. These sheets emit a thin layer of toilet paper dust as sheets are pulled off the roll. The employee suggestion box is flooded with complaints about the toilet paper, but Kevin Kramer isn't concerned. This kind of reaction is to be expected from employees who realize on a subconscious level they are about to be purged.

The executives are also not concerned. After all, Kevin Kramer had done wonders for the other companies listed on his impressive résumé. It was just a matter of time until his unorthodox magic worked. One executive said, "Kramer is either a genius or a madman. Either way, when he leaves, I'm taking his chair."

This executive later received an e-mail from Kevin Kramer with nothing in it except for a photo of Kim Kardashian and the words "Isn't she your cousin?"

During this period, the suggestion box is dismantled. An e-mail goes out to employees, saying to forward all suggestions to kkrocks@gmail.com. Only a few employees are foolish enough to send their suggestions, and soon afterward they are reassigned to part-time status. Kevin Kramer is certain these are the employees whom the executives, when surveyed, called "dumber than dirt."

Kevin Kramer likes to work as late as he can into the evening. He often misses dinner with his family, and spends hours online shopping for presents for his wife to make up for never being home. He pauses on the engagement ring section of the Tiffany website. He sometimes watches Jenna working diligently at her desk, and wonders what she would say if presented with a three-carat solitaire engagement ring in a Tiffany-blue box. He imagines her eyes widening, and can envision her jumping up and down with excitement. He can practically see the tears running down her soft, young, tanned face, smearing her perfectly applied Maybelline mascara.

Occasionally, Kevin Kramer will look at online photos of narwhals, the rare unicorn whales he remembers reading about as a child.

People have begun parking illegally in Kevin Kramer's parking space. Initially, HR sent out e-mails telling employees to move their cars, but they went unheeded. Kevin Kramer started calling the towing company himself to remove the offending vehicles.

Kevin Kramer hires expensive consultants as "usability experts." He explains to the executives that before any of the company's software goes out to the marketplace, it will have to pass muster with the usability experts. Some in the executive team argue that all the software is by definition supposed to be usable, but because they fear Kevin Kramer's wrath, they back down. Kevin Kramer hires his neighbor Karl, an unemployed soap opera actor, and Karl's brother-in-law to be the usability experts. Kevin Kramer broached the subject to Karl at a neighborhood Fourth of July party.

"How much are you paying?" Karl asked.

"I don't know, like two hundred dollars an hour? That seems right to me," said Kevin.

"Can my brother-in-law Jay get in on the action? He's not too popular with my sister lately since she found out he's been spending seven hundred dollars a month on porn sites."

"Sure, the more the merrier," Kevin said, taking a swig of his Miller Lite. Kevin Kramer only drinks light beer when he drinks beer at all.

By the end of the third quarter, Jon Goldfarb is unhappy with the products profit centers' performance. Seventy-five percent of clients surveyed indicated that customer service has gone downhill, and 80 percent say that they planned on using a competitor in the next twelve months. He meets Kevin Kramer over steaks to discuss the situation.

"As much as we can't stand our employees and, for that matter, our clients, it is our job to take care of them," Jon Goldfarb says. "It's nothing personal; it's business."

"People need to learn to take care of themselves," Kevin Kramer says. "It's our job to take care of the company. We can't be enablers."

"But we're a service company," Jon Goldfarb says.

"We need to take care of the company, in spite of the service," Kevin Kramer says, taking a bite of his porterhouse.

Kevin Kramer realizes that his time at the company is drawing to a close. His ideas have gone mostly unappreciated. His cost-cutting measures, while having worked a little, have created poor morale among the employees. The walls of the products profit center are banged up, given that employees have moved desks a number of times. Someone spray-painted a pentagram on Kevin Kramer's parking space placard.

Kevin Kramer decides it's time for a game changer. He gathers all the managers into the conference room and demands that each one of them give an extemporaneous two-minute speech on why they should be allowed to keep their jobs. A few break down in tears. More than one asks what "extemporaneous" means. Some beg for Kevin Kramer not to fire them, citing family problems and undiagnosed bipolar disorder. Several walk out in disgust and tender their resignations. Overnight, someone spray-paints the word "pussy" on the desks of those former employees. Thirty-two percent suspect it is Kevin Kramer, but 43 percent think that Kevin Kramer put one of the usability experts up to it.

Kevin Kramer receives this message on his voice mail: "Hi Kevin Kramer! You're a wanker!" Kevin Kramer will have a sneaking suspicion that it is his former assistant Debi, faking a British accent.

One morning, Kevin Kramer arrives early to work to find that someone left a poop on his desk. Twenty-eight percent of employees surveyed believed that the person, whomever it was, squatted on Kevin Kramer's desk and pooped, while 35 percent believed the person brought the poop in from a separate location.

HR sends out a memo to remaining employees, requesting that they please refrain from pooping on Kevin Kramer's desk. They will have to send out a subsequent e-mail a few days later, requesting that employees refrain from pooping on Kevin Kramer's Beemer.

Jon Goldfarb takes an extended leave of absence, leaving Kevin Kramer to deal with day-to-day company operations. By this time, Kevin Kramer has let go of most of the products profit center staff and has not hired any new people. He turns on his computer only to surf the Internet for gifts for his family. He realizes his son will turn eleven soon, eleven being the age that Kevin Kramer's parents bought him his first Time Life book about marine mammals.

Kevin Kramer wonders what would have happened if he had followed his first love. Would he be a captain on a research boat, jetting out to the warm waters of Baja, California, to study humpback whales? Would he be saving the endangered right whales found in the Atlantic and off the coast of Australia? Kevin Kramer refrains from asking himself why he has so much compassion for marine life and none for his colleagues.

Kevin Kramer quietly contacts corporate headhunters, letting them know he is looking for a new job. He lines up a few breakfast interviews for after the holidays. Kevin tells his wife he's thinking about leaving the company, but that she shouldn't worry. He will find something within a matter of weeks, as he always does. Kevin then uncharacteristically spends an hour playing Barbies with his daughter, saying in a high-pitched Barbie voice, "I hope Ken asks me to the prom!"

Kevin Kramer's wife watches her husband and daughter playing together. She hopes the children won't be too upset when they leave Kevin Kramer home while they visit her parents in Florida for the holidays. Kevin Kramer said he had too much work to do and needed to stay in town this year. Every year, Kevin Kramer says he needs to stay in town due to too much work. His son surprises him this year by saying, "Have a nice Christmas, Dad," before he can even tell the kids the news.

The day before Christmas Eve, Jenna tells Kevin Kramer that she'd like a word with him. She sits on the edge of his antique desk and tells him she's leaving the company.

"My boyfriend and I are moving to Portland," she says. "It's a lot more relaxed in Portland; the people are cooler and not so judgmental."

"I didn't know you had a boyfriend," Kevin Kramer says. "You only mentioned a cat."

"I really liked working for you," Jenna says. "If you don't mind me saying so, a lot of people here thought you were an idiot, but I think you're an expert in business. Business is a freak show, right? You do whatever you need to do in order to survive. It's like evolution—survival of the fittest."

"It can be," Kevin Kramer says.

"I'm sure you will make this company great, eventually, maybe," Jenna says. "I can't wait to apply the principles I've learned here. I bet I'll be a big success in Portland."

"I'm sure you'll knock 'em dead," Kevin Kramer says.

Jenna slides off the desk and retires to her cubicle. After she leaves for the night, Kevin Kramer walks aimlessly through the empty products profit center. The ficus trees have been dead for a while, as everyone in facilities was let go and no one else bothered to water the plants.

Kevin Kramer wonders for not the first time in his long, esteemed career if he could grow fins out of his hands and feet, and sprout a tail. He would drive his BMW to the beach and shimmy his way into the cold water. Only then could he imagine his best life, frolicking in the waves off the Pacific coast—careless, happy, and free.

An Invitation

FROM: CAITLEV@ROADRUNNER.NET
TO: UNDISCLOSED RECIPIENTS

Greetings from a stranger who is soon to be a friend!

I am Vanessa Levine's sister, Caitlin. You may be surprised to hear Vanessa has a sister. That's because Vanessa doesn't usually mention me to her friends, colleagues, or acquaintances. So while it isn't my favorite thing to e-mail a bunch of women and one guy who have no idea I exist (davedickerson@gmail.com, I assume you're an XY?), I'm writing for a very important reason. As you surely know, since you're her closest friends (or so my mother tells me), Vanessa is getting married. To celebrate this exciting milestone, I have decided to throw her a bridal shower, and you made it onto the invite list. Congratulations!

You might be thinking, *Hang on, I've already attended Vanessa's wedding shower*. That's because apparently she's already had two. Maybe you were at the shower Lola threw. Lola is Vanessa's maid of honor, even though they only met last year at a yoga retreat. I was not at that shower. I guess my invite got lost in the mail, along with the other one.

My mother, who did receive an invite, said that Lola's shower had a yoga theme. On top of that, the entertainment was a woman named Sparkle who gave everybody henna tattoos. It's ironic because I would have done those tattoos at a way reduced price. I know Sparkle. She may come off as ultra boho, but she totally overcharges. The woman drives a Tesla—I saw it once. Lola, as I know you are on this e-mail chain, FYI: now that you know I exist, please consider me for your future henna tattoo needs. I'm also a certified gemologist.

My shower is going to be way better than any of the other ones. There will be no drinking games, like the shower Vanessa's boss threw for her at Bumpers (during happy hour? So tacky!), no stupid yoga poses (no offense, Lola), and no tedious punchbowl conversation. Unless someone wants to bring a punchbowl and make punch to put in it! Who doesn't like punch?

This shower is going to be so different. I'm calling it the "Anti-Shower." Here are the deets: It's happening this Saturday at one P.M. at Vanessa's house. I'd throw it at my house, but I don't have one. I am currently living with my parents (long story, ask me about it at the Anti-Shower). Since Vanessa and her fiancé, Ken, just moved into a new house (a darling three-bedroom, two-bath midcentury modern, according to my mother), I thought, *Why not throw the shower there?* Contrary to popular belief, and my elementary school Scantron tests, I'm terrific at problem-solving.

I recognize that this is short notice, as Saturday is only two days from now, but I just had a killer therapy session and decided I have to pull the trigger on this. If I put it off any longer, I may start thinking too much about Vanessa's narcissistic personality and lose all enthusiasm for throwing her a big party. My therapist, Dr. Susan, endorses the idea. Dr. Susan has helped me immensely, and she needs only another few thousand hours to become a licensed clinician. If you are interested in her services (she's also a certified gemologist), please talk to me about it at the Anti-Shower. Anyway, I assume everyone will cancel their preexisting plans to celebrate dear Vanessa's (hopefully) one-time walk down the aisle.

Besides, I can't do it next Saturday anyways. I signed up for a screenwriting seminar, which looks awesome—it's called "How to Write an Awesome Screenplay." I was able to talk my mother into paying for it, so there is literally no way I can flake out. If you know my mother at all, then you know that she will hold that kind of thing over my head until the end of time.

The reason I'm taking this seminar is because I have an amazing idea for a film adaptation of Cheryl Strayed's book *Wild*. If you haven't heard about it, it's a memoir about how Cheryl freaked out, left her husband, and hiked by herself from L.A. to Portland via the Pacific Crest Trail. I heard about it on a rerun of *The View*. I know there's a movie out there already, but mine is going to include puppets and stop motion animation, which I am sure will pique Cheryl's interest. She needs to see the Cheryl puppet I mocked up. It's seriously cute! Her backpack talks!

BTW—if any of you know Cheryl, please extend this Anti-Shower invitation to her. So what if she has no idea who Vanessa is? I'd so love to meet her and tell her about how I too was on a downward emotional spiral for a long time and fell victim to toxic relationships. Cheryl's were marred by infidelity, enabling behavior, and drug abuse. I serially dated drummers from heavy metal cover bands. To this day, if I'm in Trader Joe's and hear "Rock You Like a Hurricane," I have to abandon my cart and leave.

Now if I'm going to pull off this shower, I'm going to need everyone's help. Here's the schedule I came up with for Saturday—please do not ask me to deviate from it. I'm going to have enough to do, and I don't need "Vanessa friends" e-mailing me with logistical problems. Solve it among yourselves, people.

According to my mother, Vanessa will be at Crunch on Saturday morning from nine to eleven, taking a Zumba class. Good for her for trying to lose that pesky muffin top! My mother has been gushing about how trim Vanessa is getting, yet she won't give me a straight answer when I ask her if my new romper makes me look fat. I think we all know what that means. I'd probably be great at Zumba—I've had strangers tell me I'm coordinated. But there's no way I can take a class. I get nauseous when people near me sweat. It's gross. Great, I just gagged a little. Let's move on.

Anyway, I will need a volunteer to meet me at Vanessa's house promptly at nine. Ideally, that volunteer will know where Vanessa's house is because I might not be able to get the address out of my mother. It would be helpful too if this person has the key. And also bring a Swiffer, because I'm sure we're going to have to Lysol that place hard. We all know Vanessa's a slob—haha—but is it that funny? My future brother-in-law, Ken, must be someone who grew up with poor housekeeping habits. Maybe he was raised in a commune. Now I'm thinking I'll need at least three volunteers. Solve it among yourselves, people.

I just met Ken a week ago when I randomly ran into him and Vanessa at Target. He seemed pretty shocked to find out that Vanessa had a sister. He kept staring at me and then back at Vanessa—awkward! The first thing my mother told me about Ken is that he's a patent attorney who makes a ton of money, so in other words, he's perfect for Vanessa. The first thing I noticed about him is that he has a lot of arm hair. I'm so happy they found each other.

The toilet paper aisle at Target is not an ideal place to meet one's new brother-in-law. Vanessa even pretended not to see me at first. She was all like, "I didn't recognize you with your head shaved on one side." She recognized me all right—I was wearing her prom dress. I found it in the closet of her old bedroom, next to a Wham! poster (really?). Some people can't pull off pink taffeta for running errands, but based on the looks Ken was giving me, I rocked it!

Also, I'm going to need to know some things before I decorate Vanessa's living room—like if she has a living room. Someone on this e-mail chain must have been to her house before. Please sketch the layout and send it to me so I can get my decor dimensions straight. Did I mention I am applying to be a contestant on a new reality show, *America's Next Top Event Planner*? It is crucial that the decorations look fantastic, because I need to use the photos for my application. Did I mention it's due in a week?

This reminds me, does someone have an HD camera they can bring to the shower? My flip phone takes crappy photos, and without good ones, my chances of winning *America's Next Top Event Planner* will be slim. It's the reason I got rejected from *The Next Top Nature Photographer*. Who's going to watch that anyway?

While we're on the subject, I am going to use three of you as references on my application. I picked people who have legit-sounding e-mail addresses. No offense, Lola, but yogagrll@aol.com is so 2006.

My future is riding on this, so please help a girl out. If the producers contact you, give me a stellar recommendation. Say that I am easy to work with. Say that I take clients' suggestions seriously. Say that I planned your dad's retirement brunch and that it was beyond festive. Say that I designed your daughter's bat mitzvah with a sea mammal theme, and that the rabbi raved about the chopped liver mold shaped like a porpoise.

Back to the shower! I've got an amazing design aesthetic planned. It's both eco-friendly and affordable. I'm using materials that have either been plucked from the earth or stolen from dumpsters. I'm branding myself as *the* event planner for those on a micro-budget. Poor people have events worth celebrating too! I think it's a genuinely marketable concept.

There are several large-scale conceptual pieces that I am in the process of glue-gunning together. Once they dry, we will mount them on Vanessa's walls using two-by-fours. (Dave Dickerson, how tall are you? Can you lift more than fifty pounds? Have you ever used a drill saw?)

Also, I found this fantastic wagon-wheel chandelier that someone left out on the curb and a bunch of troll dolls that a neighbor chucked out. I also pilfered through my mother's Goodwill pile and found some stained old tablecloths. I dyed them using tea and crushed-up American Spirit cigarettes, and they turned out really vintage-y. Now I just need to figure out how to cover up the smell. Come to think of it, we might get pretty stinky doing all this decorating. I'm sure Vanessa won't mind if we use her shower. (Don't worry, Dave, I promise I won't peek under your towel!)

But what if we damage Vanessa's walls or home in general? you might be asking. No problem, I've already thought of that—this is America's Next Top Event Planner talking, after all. We'll go to Ken, tell him we were only trying to make his future wife happy, and ask him to cover the damages. We'll remind him that home repairs are a tax write-off! At least I think they are.

I'm concerned that with all this decorating, we may run out of time before Vanessa gets home from the gym. That's why I'm troubleshooting the situation, *ANTEP* style! I've asked my mother to meet Vanessa outside the locker room at Crunch and say they both need to have mani-pedis right away. Don't worry, that won't seem weird. My mother is famous for demanding emergency mani-pedis.

There is a chance my mother will back out. She might say that her fibromyalgia is acting up and she can't use her fingers without terrible pain (her usual lame excuse when I ask for her help). If so, then I have a plan B. Someone will need to meet Vanessa and say they need her help with a big problem. It can be anybody but Dave Dickerson because I need him to lift stuff. Dave, it's been a long time since I had someone around who would help me with chores. I never thought about what a bummer it is to do things like take out the trash until I had to do it by myself. It's enough to make a person stop taking out the trash altogether and find reasons to keep their trash instead. On the positive side, last week's moldy bread is adding a great textural component to one of my wall pieces!

What to say to Vanessa? Make something up. You could tell her you got a nasty call from your former landlady, saying your credit card was declined when she tried to charge last month's rent. You tried telling her that you were waiting for some T.J. Maxx credits to come through, so could she run it again in a week? When she responded with profanity, you tried explaining that you would soon be winning a major reality show whose top prize would surely total more than the nine hundred bucks she was bugging you for. Say your former landlady is a real asshole and her name is Bonnie Driscoll.

Under no circumstances should you mention my name or this shower. It will freak Vanessa out. I think most of you can probably tell from this e-mail that Vanessa and I are not the closest of sisters. For some reason, she has always been paranoid that I'm trying to humiliate her. What kind of person thinks that way about her baby sister? What bad thing did I ever do to her that wasn't accidental? I pose this question to you all: Which sister do you think suffers from narcissistic personality disorder and is badly in need of treatment? Hint: I'm already in treatment with Dr. Susan, remember?

Onward to the food: since I am already scheduling, designing, and implementing this event, I'm going to need you to solve that one among yourselves. One of you must know how to cook. Or how to order food from a caterer and pay for it. We can all pitch in, but I'm going to have to pay in T.J. Maxx extra bucks. (Heads up—extra bucks can only be used on sale-priced items, excluding JLo glassware.) Working part-time at T.J. Maxx does have its perks!

Please plan on enough food for fifty people. Leftovers will not go to waste. I found a pan flute club willing to entertain for free, and I'm sure most of them don't eat on a regular basis. I went to one of their meetings, and someone brought in doughnuts. If you've ever seen one of those National Geographic specials where a pack of hyenas devour a zebra, then you'll get the picture. (Dave Dickerson, quick off-topic question—how exactly do you know Vanessa? Do you work with her in the finance department? If so, are you single? I'm used to dating musicians, and they can be sort of hard to depend on.)

Let me suggest some options for food and bev. I'm envisioning a "Food from the 1960s Soviet Union" theme, so just bring caviar blini, bacon-wrapped dates, borscht, and flavored vodka erupting from an ice sculpture shaped like the Kremlin. I think they can do something like that at Trader Joe's.

Regarding the cake: Costco is great for ten-gallon drums of peanut butter, but not for a wedding shower cake. Please order from a real bakery. One idea is the chocolate cake with banana filling from Sweet Lady Jane. It's my favorite. I bet for a little extra cash, they would decorate it like the USSR flag, whatever that looks like. Someone google it.

I need another volunteer to make sure Ken does not come home at all on Saturday. Does anyone know what he does on weekends? Can we get him to go into work? Can someone pay for him to go to Vegas? I am sure he enjoys drinking, watching sports, and going to strip clubs. (Dave Dickerson, do you like strip clubs? Do you like the kind where girls strip or boys strip? Meow! Dave, another question: Generally speaking, do you hate taking out the trash? Or are you willing to do it now and again, that is, if you lived with someone in a monogamous relationship?)

Can anyone provide me with Ken's number so I can discuss this with him myself? I have tried to get it from my mother, but she is refusing to answer my texts and won't come out of her bedroom. I can't ask Vanessa for it because she won't give me her number. Also, she'd probably get all paranoid that I would try to steal Ken for myself.

Ever since I accidentally fellated her college boyfriend when she brought him home for Thanksgiving, she has not trusted me. Accidents happen, Vanessa, geez. Plus, it's been twenty years, isn't it time to let it go already? Anyway, from what I've seen of Ken, she has nothing to worry about. He looks like my father. I wonder what Dr. Susan would say about that. Why would Vanessa seek out a hairier version of my father? Someone google it.

I think it's obvious by now that Vanessa and I approach life in completely different ways. Blindly following the straight and narrow path might make a person appear successful in one's parents' estimation and among one's bestest friends at a yoga retreat (no offense, Lola), but it does not necessarily make one a good person. Just like drinking too much at Thanksgiving dinner and orally pleasing one's sister's boyfriend in the garage doesn't make one a bad person.

When did I become the bad sister? Vanessa never looked out for me when we were kids. We'd ride the bus to junior high together, and when Tom Weed spit in my hair, she laughed along with all the other kids and the bus driver. If you think about it, that kind of behavior speaks volumes about a person's moral compass. And trust me, that's not my only horror story from growing up with Vanessa. She didn't talk to me the whole first semester of my sophomore year, just because I refused to wear a bra (or brush my teeth) for political reasons. That, my friends, is not only mean-spirited, but antifeminist.

To use the analogy I gave Dr. Susan, I see myself as Barbra Streisand in *The Way We Were,* my all-time favorite movie. Babs and I are both outsiders; in fact, we're trailblazers, yearning for that WASP god Hubbell Gardiner. (Dave Dickerson, are you a WASP?) BTW—what the hell happened to Robert Redford's face? Was it too much sun? It's just not fair.

Do you know what Vanessa's favorite movie is? *Dirty Dancing*. Gimme a break. Who does she think she is,

Jennifer Grey? A plucky cutie-pie who improbably seduces the hot dance instructor and saves the day? Well, news flash: taking beginner Zumba and marrying a hairy patent attorney is not the same thing. Not to mention, Baby is the younger sister! The older sister was vapid, nasty to Baby, and only interested in snagging a rich guy. Here's one last thing I'll say about it: Jennifer Grey = nose fixed, winner of *Dancing with the Stars*. Barbra Streisand = nose not fixed, American legend.

Which brings me to the gifts: absolutely no gifts are allowed at the Anti-Shower. If someone shows up with one, I will order them to put it back in the trunk of their hybrid SUV. Besides, last I checked, most of the items on Vanessa's registries were already purchased, except for an Oreck Magnesium vacuum that costs $800 (really?).

Vanessa doesn't cook, she can't stand entertaining, and she can barely do the laundry, so why she needs china and serving forks and coffee service for thirty-six is beyond me. No, the only gifts accepted at this shower will be charitable donations. I ask that you consider giving the donations to me to cover the financial and emotional burdens of putting on this shower. Also, these monies may very well ensure that I become a reality star and might possibly meet Cheryl Strayed on the set of a talk show. These are things that can only help Vanessa and Ken in the long run. Consider it.

I'm starting to get super excited about this shower! Initially, I would have rather ripped off a hangnail than plan a party for Vanessa. But I can see now just how important it is for me to follow through. My parents are getting older and won't be around forever. Eventually, it will be just Vanessa and me left, without our parents around to keep us abreast of each other's successes and failures, although I have to admit that might be a relief. It is vital that Vanessa and I put our issues behind us and forge a more grown-up relationship. Will I be able to forgive her for begging me to play Monopoly with her when we were kids, only to quit the moment I landed on Boardwalk? Can I let go of the fact that all of my friends liked her better because she showed them the dirty pages in Judy Blume's *Forever . . .* ? Can I get over that she graduated cum laude from Berkeley, while I struggled in school due to impulse control issues? (Dave, I need to know: Are you an alcoholic? If so, this will never work between us.) Forgiving Vanessa will be a tall order, but all I can do is try. This Anti-Shower is going to be a glorious new beginning for Vanessa and me. I can only hope that Vanessa will appreciate the hoops I'm jumping through to make it happen. Maybe she'll even return my e-mails once in a while. Or accept my friend request on Facebook.

So that's the plan! If I don't hear back from you, then I'll see you at Vanessa's house bright and early on Saturday morning. Please check your attitudes at the door, as I want to get through the day with as little drama as possible. I've been under a great deal of stress lately, what with losing most of my T.J. Maxx hours (long story, nothing to do with check fraud). Also, my parents are trying to force me out of the house and into a sober living residence using techniques they learned from watching *Hoarders*.

Put yourselves in my shoes. Some of you must have sisters. Think about how great you would feel if you could do something nice for her. Maybe for once she would stop acting like you were some huge fuckup she can barely tolerate. She might celebrate your successes, no matter how minor they might seem, like when you apprenticed with a henna tattoo artist, or signed up for a screenwriting seminar. She might show up on your birthday with a cake from Sweet Lady Jane instead of never calling or sending a card. Maybe she'd even want you to be the maid of honor at her wedding (no offense, Lola). Maybe one time, you'd hear from her out of the blue, just to check in. That could happen. Maybe she'd say, "Caitlin, I need a manicure in the worst way," and even though she didn't come right out and say it, you'd know that out of everyone in the whole world, you were the first person she thought of to call.

Onset

DR. MARCH'S WAITING ROOM IS DECORATED IN an Old World, Oriental style. The chairs look like they should be covered in plastic. The art on the walls looks like something your grandparents would have brought back from a trip to Hong Kong in the 1960s: framed prints of brown waves washing up onto a brown shore. There is pro-Israeli literature printed off the Internet on the coffee table in Dr. March's waiting room where there should be magazines. There are elderly people sitting with you in the waiting room. A few remind you of your grandparents, but your grandparents have been gone for a long time. You might be older now than you remember your grandparents being back when you were a small child.

In Dr. March's examining room, there is a picture hanging on the wall next to Dr. March's various medical degrees. It is a line drawing of two old Jewish men from the old country, one carrying a hen. There is a caption underneath the old Jewish men that reads "A Chicken for Every Pot." This too is a picture that you might have seen hanging on the living room wall of your grandparents' apartment on the North Side of Chicago. This kind of painting should have a gilt frame. You begin to wonder whether you are in Dr. March's examining room or in your grandparents' living room.

Dr. March is busy. He doesn't look up while you are talking. He asks if you still have pain in your hands, because the last time you were in to see him, you had pain in your hands. You cannot remember what kind of hand pain you complained about last time. You look at your hands. You wiggle your fingers. You bend your hands at the wrist.

"There's no pain," you say. Dr. March does not seem surprised.

You remind Dr. March that you are not here about your hands. You are here about your back. You have lower back pain. You do not know what is causing it. Dr. March orders you to stand up. He asks you to bend over and touch your toes. He presses on your back. You do not have any pain at all. You tell Dr. March that the pain comes on at night, that you wake up at night with pain in your lower back. Dr. March asks if you have gained weight. Dr. March has your chart right in front of him, so he knows what you weighed the last time you were in to see him, when you complained about the pain in your hands, and he knows how much you weigh today. He knows that you have gained weight, but still, he asks you, "So, well, have you gained weight?" You have to answer yes; otherwise, you'd be lying. Dr. March says that gaining weight says something about a person's state of mind. Dr. March says that as people age and gain weight, it is a recipe for many other health problems, like diabetes. And back pain.

Dr. March says that there is nothing wrong with your back. He says that you should call him if your insurance situation improves so that he can do some tests on you. He says you should call him if you still have pain in a few weeks. He does not mention what kind of pain.

You want to explain that you are coming to see him, Dr. March, out of network because he is your last hope. The other doctors you have seen in your HMO have not helped you. All you have gotten is a referral for another doctor, an orthopedic doctor, who examined you and told you that there was nothing wrong with your back that a little exercise couldn't cure. When you went back to your main HMO doctor, she looked at you in a hard way and said that she could give you a referral for a psychiatrist. You have been down that road before, but you let her refer you to the psychiatrist anyway. You haven't yet made an appointment.

You want to explain to Dr. March that that is why you are here, paying out of your own pocket so that you do not have to make an appointment with the psychiatrist. But Dr. March is busy and on to the next patient.

Dr. March's nurse Ronnie is a nice woman. She reminds you of the maiden daughter of the elderly woman who lived in the apartment next to your grandparents' on the North Side. She's the kind of woman who, from her elderly mother's kitchen window on the second floor, would see visitors walking through the main apartment building door, and then would knock on your grandparents' door to see who had come over. She might bring over a large piece of coffee cake that she had baked that morning, the kind with streusel on top.

Dr. March barks orders to Ronnie; Ronnie faxes papers, takes phone calls, and talks to patients. You envision Ronnie in her snow boots and ski hat, shoveling off the front stoop of her mother's apartment building during the wintertime. You can see Ronnie making her elderly mother a cup of tea. You can see Ronnie in her elderly mother's tiny kitchen, sitting at the tiny kitchen table, peeling carrots into a bowl.

Ronnie tells you that lower back pain is common. She tells you that she sees a lot of people coming in to see Dr. March with back pain. She tells you that the wet, cold weather can cause joint pain. You can see yourself having a similar conversation with Ronnie, even if she wasn't Dr. March's nurse. You can picture yourself sitting at your grandparents' dining room table, across from Ronnie, stirring a cup of tea.

Ronnie's hair is bright red, except the roots along her part are gray. As Ronnie speaks from across her desk, you watch a flush pass across her face. For a moment her eyes shine with joy and she is impossibly beautiful. You wonder why Ronnie never married. You wonder what Ronnie thinks about while cleaning up after her elderly mother, while she lovingly passes a comb across her elderly mother's tender scalp.

In between faxing papers and talking on the phone, Ronnie asks after your husband, and you answer that you do not have a husband. Ronnie looks at you in a funny way—her eyebrows go up and down, and the youthful flush you noticed earlier on her cheeks seems to disappear. You can see the wrinkles on Ronnie's neck, like a chicken's neck. Ronnie says that she thought you had a husband, but that she must have been thinking of someone else.

You are taking up too much of Ronnie's time, but each time you think it is the right time to leave, you linger. Ronnie's coworkers are giving you looks that say, *Go away, you old hen! You should be the chicken in the pot!* But you want to stay; you want to talk to Ronnie, to pretend that you are chatting over a cup of tea while the wind howls outside. You ask Ronnie if she used to live in Chicago and she looks at you funny.

"No," she says, "no, I'm a California girl, lived here all my life."

You want to tell Ronnie that she somehow makes you think of your grandparents' apartment, of the wintery stoop and the warm coffee cake and the gilt frames and plastic furniture coverings of years ago, but she is busy, so you bite your tongue.

After a week, the lower back pain has not gone away, but rather has migrated to the side of your head, behind your right eye. You do not feel the pain behind your eye all the time, but if you think about it, you can feel the pain lurking there, waiting to be felt. You call Dr. March's office. You ask for Ronnie and are put on hold. When she finally picks up, you tell her about the eye pain that you are about to have. You tell her that every second you are waiting, expectantly, for your eye to begin hurting. Ronnie listens to your story, and she clucks her tongue over and over again. You can imagine Ronnie clucking that way over a story you would tell her while sitting at your grandparents' dining table. It would be the story about your cousin Harriet, the one who became schizophrenic suddenly at the age of twenty and who lived for years in her parents' basement, rarely venturing outside. She was such a promising young lady, you would tell Ronnie; she played the piano so beautifully. Ronnie would roll her eyes up to the heavens, cluck her tongue, and then ask if you wanted the recipe for her coffee cake, the kind with the streusel on top. You would tell Ronnie that you were never much for baking, and she would laugh and say, *Just follow the recipe*. You would mention that your apartment has an old stove and that you can't be sure of how anything is going to turn out. Ronnie would laugh again and say, *Old stoves cook as well as new stoves*.

You notice that Ronnie hasn't said anything on the phone for a few minutes while you talk about your cousin Harriet. When you speak into the receiver, there is no one there.

You make the appointment to see the psychiatrist. The psychiatrist you meet with is a man. He is not an attractive man, but he looks at you while you talk. He is not like Dr. March, who is busy and has no time for you. This doctor has brown eyes and an Indian name. While you are talking to him, you wonder if he can understand English. He nods and writes with a ballpoint pen into a notebook. You try to make out what he is writing, but you can't discern any of the words. You wonder if the doctor is writing in a different language.

You tell the psychiatrist about the back pain that has migrated to your eye. You tell the psychiatrist that you have gained some weight over the last few years. You ask the psychiatrist if he knows Dr. March. You tell the doctor about Dr. March's waiting room, about the furnishings and the pictures hanging on the wall and the pro-Israeli literature on the coffee table where magazines should be. You tell the psychiatrist that being in Dr. March's waiting room feels familiar, like being in your grandparents' apartment. The psychiatrist writes it all down. The psychiatrist asks if you have been sleeping. You tell the psychiatrist that sometimes, when you think you are awake, like when you are talking on the phone, it seems like you fall asleep, and when you come to your senses, you find that the person on the other end of the line has hung up.

"We all get hung up on every so often," he says, laughing a little.

The psychiatrist asks if you are married. You tell him no. He looks at you funny and asks if you have ever been married. You tell him no, that for many years, you lived near your mother on the North Side. You tell him that you took care of your elderly mother and shoveled her stoop during the long winters, and peeled potatoes and carrots for the cabbage soup that your elderly mother still insisted on making, even though hardly anyone visited anymore. You tell the psychiatrist how you combed your mother's white hair. You told the psychiatrist that you used to be beautiful, but that no one notices you anymore. You told him how you used to dye your hair red until the roots started coming in faster, and then you stopped. You tell him about how you work for Dr. March now, that you fax documents and help patients.

The psychiatrist writes faster, trying to get all the words onto the page as you are speaking. You feel a flush pass along your cheeks, and you feel as though you must be beautiful. The psychiatrist says that the hour is up. You stand up to leave. The doctor says that you might want to think about losing some weight. The doctor says that he wants to see you back next week. The doctor gives you three prescriptions for pills and instructs you to get them filled right away. The doctor asks if, in the meantime, there is anyone who calls to check up on you. You tell him that you have a friend named Ronnie whom you speak to every so often.

Ronnie returns your call from the day before. You do not remember calling her the day before, but you are happy to hear from her. You feel touched that Ronnie called you herself, instead of getting one of the girls in the office to call you, the girls in the office who snicker behind your back. You can always tell when someone is snickering about you behind your back.

"Are you okay, hon?" Ronnie asks you. "Because we're worried about you over here."

You assure Ronnie that you are fine; you tell Ronnie that you went to see a psychiatrist.

You ask Ronnie if she's ever made coffee cake with streusel topping. She laughs and says, "Maybe one time, a long time ago." You ask Ronnie how her mother is faring, if she is still alive after all these years. There is a pause on the line, and then Ronnie asks you the name of the psychiatrist you are seeing. You find the paper you wrote the appointment down on, and you tell Ronnie the doctor's name. The psychiatrist's name is Fincher, but you tell Ronnie that you were certain he was an Indian doctor. You tell Ronnie that when you tried to read his notes and the prescriptions that he wrote for you, you were certain that he was writing in a foreign language. You tell Ronnie that he wrote in strange curlicues, in upside-down numbers and letters, and that you could make neither heads nor tails of it.

Ronnie says that you should come in for an appointment immediately, that Dr. March wants to do some tests on you. You don't tell Ronnie this, but you cannot afford to have the tests that Dr. March wants you to have. You can only have the tests that the HMO allows you to have. You tell Ronnie that you will be there, that you've written down the appointment date and time, and that you wouldn't miss seeing her for the world. But you haven't written down the appointment. You won't remember when it is. Ronnie says, "I'm hanging up now, so you hang up too," and when you start to say that you are hanging up, you hear that Ronnie has already hung up.

After you hang up the phone, you wonder if Ronnie has dyed her roots red, or if they are still gray. You wonder if Ronnie's elderly mother still has the picture of the men from the old country and the chicken hanging in the living room of her apartment. You wonder if you can still remember the recipe for your mother's cabbage soup. You wonder if Ronnie will be the one to run a comb across your tender white scalp when the time comes. You listen for the wind outside, but you can't hear anything but waves, quietly lapping against a brown shore.

Him

IT'S VERY DIFFICULT TO STAY PURE IN THIS WORLD. The devil hides in places where you'd never think to look, like in the back row of our department meetings, or crouching behind the urinal in the men's room. I've even felt his hellfire through the mesh seat of my Aeron chair.

When I see the devil, I silently mouth the words "You will be vanquished." I can't say it out loud anymore since HR put out that memo: "While worship is a necessary part of many employees' lives, it will not be permitted in the building. Please limit all prayer activity to the patio."

Admonishing sin is my duty, because I believe in Him. I am a founding member of a group called the People Who Believe in Him, and by Him, You Know Who We Mean. We also considered the name Believers in Him, but it sounded grammatically weird.

The People Who Believe in Him, and by Him, You Know Who We Mean is comprised of me and my brother, Jesse. We are an island haven in a big, horrible sea of Nonbelievers.

My office is full of Nonbelievers, except for a few people like Gina. She works downstairs in residuals. Gina used to be a lesbian, but she became a Believer and gave up her lesbian ways. We met praying on the patio.

Even though Gina had five girlfriends in the past and some boyfriends too, and has her tongue pierced, she considers herself a do-over virgin. She says that He has cleansed her of all of her sins. Isn't it awesome that He can transform a former dyke who was for sure going to Hell into a model of virtue and purity? I would never say that to Gina, though, because I don't want to offend a Believer. But it is awesome!

I have to socialize with Nonbelievers pretty regularly, like at happy hour after work at Duffy's. Hanging out with Nonbelievers sucks because there's no one to talk about virtue with, or about how cool we think He is. One time, when the Kings game was on at Duffy's and they scored, I shouted, "Praise Him!" A few of my coworkers snickered.

I guess it's not politically correct to glorify Him in a bar full of Nonbelievers. I'm sure those Nonbelievers would have a different reaction if they knew that they were going to suffer in Hell once He returns to earth and takes us Believers up with Him to Heaven.

I get suckered into attending the Nonbeliever happy hours because when my boss gets a little tipsy, she ends up paying for all of our drinks. Usually, if she's been scowling for most of the day, all anyone has to do is mention Duffy's happy hour and she gets all like "C'mon team, let's let off some steam." How can I say no?

When I go to happy hour with the People Who Believe in Him, and by Him, You Know Who We Mean, we have to order the cheapest pitchers of beer because money is always tight. And because it's just me and Jesse and we live together, we never have that much to talk about after we glorify His name.

Also, Jesse is in between jobs, so I end up paying, and Jesse can sure suck down ten-dollar pitchers of Bud Light. But at the Nonbeliever happy hours, I can order as much Sam Adams as I want, plus my boss lets us order sliders and hot wings, so I get dinner out of it too.

Regardless of how many pitchers my boss buys, it won't change the fact that she's still a Nonbeliever and going to Hell. I'd like for her to see the Light and follow the Way, but I got a talking to by HR for praying too loudly on the patio during my lunch hour, so I try not to talk about Him at work anymore. It's a challenge, especially when I see the devil, dressed in office-appropriate khakis but drooling fire, hiding behind the potted ficus tree near accounts receivable.

He has to understand that due to corporate policies beyond my control, I can't save anyone at work. The Nonbelievers are going to have to figure things out by themselves or be forced to spend eternity in fire and damnation. It's not impossible—Gina, the former lesbian in residuals, did it.

I do what I can to stay true to Him at work. Example: I am nice to everybody. I don't engage in vicious gossip about my coworkers, or join in when they watch unchaste cat videos on YouTube. Example: Clients love me. They are always saying things like, "Kyle, you're the best support rep over there." I want to say, *You can praise Him instead, because all that I am is for His glory,* but it's been suggested to me that this kind of response makes some clients uncomfortable. Frankly, Nonbeliever clients should feel uncomfortable, because they're going to burn in Hell.

I'd like to help only the Believer clients, but it's hard to tell over the phone if someone is a Believer. My dad told me once how to distinguish Believers from Nonbelievers. He said that Believers bruise easier than Nonbelievers because He is in their blood.

There's a temp named Cynthia who started this week. She replaced that Asian guy who went out on disability. She's older, like in her forties. She's got frizzy hair and she wears long skirts that look like hand-me-downs from 1975. She's not attractive, but she does have these huge boobs that I notice myself staring at. Sometimes I catch her looking at me while she's making copies, so to remain pure, I try not to make too much eye contact. You know what He says: "Whosoever looketh on a woman to lust after her hath committed adultery with her already in his heart." But thinking about Cynthia's boobs makes me want to go into the men's room when no one else is in there and rub one out. As a Believer, you're never supposed to rub one out, even if you're married. And believe me, I don't.

Maybe I fudge a little bit on special days like my birthday or Christmas, although Christmas is probably not the best time to rub one out because it's His birthday. I'm not worried, though, because He knows I'm a Believer. That's the most important thing. I don't think that rubbing out a few on Christmas morning is going to keep me from getting into Heaven.

Cynthia sits in the cubicle next to me, and I swear, sometimes she smells funky, like she just attended a Grateful Dead concert. Or like maybe she sucked someone's dick before coming to work. Maybe she went down on some guy who commutes with her in the same vanpool. Maybe she makes a point to sit with him in the backseat of the van each morning while the other commuters knit or sleep in the second row, oblivious to what she's doing back there. I shouldn't be thinking about things of that nature, but in my opinion, that type of behavior would definitely warrant a discussion and a prayer vigil with the participants. He doesn't approve of premarital sexual activity, which definitely includes dick sucking. I won't be partaking of any of that until I'm married.

My future wife will only smell like my dick, and that won't be until after we're safely married. No dick sucking before that time, even if she was so horny that she could barely stand it and begged to suck my dick in the vanpool on the way to work. I bet Cynthia is a tiger in the sack!

Jesse recently got engaged to this girl named Megan whom he met on an Internet site for Believers. She is kind of chubby, but she's a real nice girl. I think she'll make Jesse a good wife in that she likes to try out recipes in her crockpot. Some of her stews taste pretty good.

I think Jesse is looking forward to getting some action once they are married, and that's probably why they pushed the wedding date up to next month. Once they get married, it will be weird to have another person in our group, especially since Megan doesn't approve of drinking alcohol, not even at happy hours. Maybe she'll just clean their apartment when Jesse and I go to Duffy's for prayers and beer. If she makes Jesse stay home, then it's going to be a pretty small group with just me in it. I may have to merge with the Believers at work, but I'm not sure how committed they are to Him, especially since I saw Gina and Tim, a guy in IT, making out in his truck in the parking lot. You're not supposed to do that. It could land you in a lot of trouble with Him. But who am I to judge? That's for Him to decide, but if you ask me, I think that Gina of all people ought to watch it. Like He says, "Can a man take fire in his bosom, and his clothes not be burned?"

Today I went to the men's room after my fifteen-minute break, and when I was coming out, I passed Cynthia going into the ladies' room.

"We're on the same schedule," she said.

I stammered out, "Hehe, right," and I tried to act natural, but then I thought maybe it was her way of trying to lure me into the ladies' room so she could smack my butt or lick my balls. I wouldn't put it past her. Then I couldn't help it, I had to go rub one out in the men's room, even though it wasn't a special occasion. I tried to be real quiet about it, although after I flushed the toilet paper with my seed on it, I'm pretty sure I heard the devil laughing from inside the new low-flow toilet.

I knelt on the cold bathroom floor and prayed that He would forgive me, and that He wouldn't be too mad that my flesh was weak. I meant to promise Him that it wouldn't happen again, but Ron from research walked in while I was kneeling, so I had to pretend that I had dropped my contact lens.

When I got back to my cubicle, I saw that my boss had left a Post-it note on my monitor. It said, "Your break is only fifteen minutes, not thirty."

I don't care that I got in trouble with my boss, so long as He doesn't come down from Heaven and leave me pissy Post-it notes.

I will have to pray extra hard on the patio for my misdeed, but I'm starting to feel like I may need to rub another one out in the men's room. That Cynthia is a Jezebel! I bet she's had hundreds of men. My dad always said that women can't resist sex the way men can, but that He forgives them more easily because they are weak in both flesh and spirit.

I wonder why He is testing me so hard when I've always been completely devoted to Him, even when I was a kid. Early one morning when I was about eight, He appeared to me at my bedroom window. He was amazing! He had flowing blond locks and bushy sideburns and wore a tunic made out of gold. In retrospect, he looked a lot like Robert Plant, but I was too young to be into Zeppelin at the time. He said to me, "You are the Bud and I am the Sun." Then He opened the window and stepped out into the sunshine.

After that, I realized that I was His servant, and that I was not to think impure thoughts or perform impure deeds until He finds me an appropriate wife to perform them on. In the meantime, I hope that He appreciates the effort I am making on His behalf because it's freaking hard! I'm sure He does. As He says, "If you have faith as small as a mustard seed, you can say to this mountain, 'Move from here to there,' and it will move. Nothing will be impossible for you." If I can move a mountain, then I should definitely be able to keep myself from rubbing one out during my fifteen-minute break.

Cynthia was filing near my desk today, and she kept staring at me with a lustful look in her eyes. I tried to keep my cool, turning my head so that I could stay focused on the clients on the phone, but she was wearing these rubber thimbles on her fingers for filing that reminded me of condoms. I tried to breathe through it and think about the NFL Draft, but it wasn't helping at all. After I got off the phone, Cynthia leaned over the partition. Her breath smelled sort of like Cool Ranch Doritos.

"You know who you look like, Kyle? My ex," Cynthia said. Up close, I could see that her eyebrows were painted on in brown pencil.

"I do?" I said.

"He always looked like he was up to something," she said with a sly grin. "Up to no good."

Every time she said the word "up," my boner got worse and worse, and I couldn't even excuse myself to go to the bathroom because everyone in the call center would see! I am starting to believe that the devil himself put Cynthia up to this. I need to concentrate more on Him. Cynthia's boobs are the work of Satan.

I met with a few other Believers praying out on the patio at lunch. We all talked about how stupid that HR memo was, and then we realized just how cool it was that we all were forced to pray in one place. It was like He engineered it so that we could all meet and glorify His name together. We decided to celebrate by going to Duffy's after work.

Initially, we had a great time, even though we had to pay for our own beer. We tried to get a booth but they were all taken. It's a lot less noticeable to hold hands and pray in a booth than it is at a table. Not that I care that the Nonbelievers at Duffy's looked at us funny and called us weirdos while we were praying. It won't be so funny once they are suffering in Hell.

Then we started talking about Him, but then Cynthia showed up and interrupted. She said, "I'm waiting for someone. Do you mind if I hang out with you guys for a bit?" I said, "We're sort of having a meeting here," but dorky Tim, the guy I've seen making out with Gina in the parking lot, said, "Everyone is welcome at our friendship circle." He made me move over so that Cynthia could squeeze in. She scooted up extremely close to me, and at a certain point I felt like she was practically on my lap. Maybe she smokes a lot of pot, because her clothes just reeked of something musky, and I noticed that her face didn't move at all when she talked and that her forehead seemed frozen. She kept looking at me with this hard expression on her face, like she was trying to take something away from me. I also couldn't stop thinking about her being on my lap, bouncing up and down on my big hard cock, her enormous breasts pressed right into my face, and I got a huge boner, right there at the table. Believers are not supposed to get hard-ons while participating in a prayer vigil! Especially if you aren't sitting in a booth, where it's easier to cover yourself up.

I couldn't even excuse myself to go to the bathroom because I was ready to bust out of my jeans. Finally, after a beer or two, Cynthia left. I was shaken, like the devil himself had traveled up from Hell to take me far away from Him.

My boss called me into her office today.

"Kyle, is everything okay with you?" she said.

"Everything's great," I said.

"Because you seem to be disappearing quite a bit. You're rarely at your desk," she said.

At first, I didn't say anything. Did she honestly think that I was going to confess my sins to her? But she had this expectant look on her face, so I had to come up with something.

"Uh, I've been in the bathroom," I said.

I didn't want to lie. He doesn't approve of lying.

"It's not my intention to embarrass you, Kyle, but if you are having digestive issues, I'm going to suggest that you make a doctor's appointment right away. It's important that you put your health first. We need you healthy." She smiled.

"I want to be healthy," I said.

Then she got a phone call, so I left. I don't know why this is happening to me. I've never had a problem resisting vice, not even in high school. Jesse would get in trouble all the time, mouthing off to teachers, smoking weed in the gym bathroom, even telling my dad to go fuck himself. I never did anything like that.

My dad would get extremely pissed off when Jesse told him to go fuck himself. One time I remember him grabbing both of Jesse's hands, saying, "We're going to pray now," and my brother tried to wrench his hands free, but my dad held on until the Spirit entered him. Then my dad pulled Jesse onto the floor, and he pulled his jeans and underwear down and started wailing on Jesse's bare butt with his fists. I remember thinking that Jesse's butt was small, like the size of my dad's two fists put together end to end. My father started shouting, "Praise Him!" and I shouted, "Praise Him!" I'm not sure how long we lasted like that, but afterward my dad wept with Jesse and said, "Justice has been done."

Unfortunately, Jesse got caught the next week with more weed in his locker, so my dad had to wail on him again. He sure works in mysterious ways.

This afternoon, Cynthia leaned over the partition between her cubicle and my cubicle, but I pretended to be editing some documents while she tried to get my attention. I wish she would take a hint.

"Hey, Kyle, would it be cool if I went to happy hour with you and your friends the next time you go?" she asked.

"Uh, it's more of a prayer group than a bunch of friends going out," I said. "Do you accept Him as your personal savior?" I asked. I don't think He would like it if we opened our circle up to Nonbelievers, especially weird, smelly ones like Cynthia. That might defeat the point.

"Sure. I mean, yeah," Cynthia said. "When are you guys going out next?"

"Tomorrow after work," I told her. "So, you completely believe in Him?" I had to ask.

Cynthia stared at me before saying, "Of course I do, silly." I wanted to question her further, but before I could say anything, she turned around to answer a phone call. Cynthia just doesn't seem like a Believer to me. Most women who are Believers are married and have grandkids by the time they get to be Cynthia's age. Most women who are Believers don't flaunt their big breasts in tiny tank tops the way Cynthia does. Most women who are Believers don't smell funky, like the way sperm smells after it's been shot out of a penis.

I went home from work that night and tried to read His Word for a few hours, but everything I was reading made me feel completely horny, even the parts that usually bore me, although I would never tell Him that any part of His Word is boring.

I got desperate and woke Jesse up and asked him to slap me a few times, so I could get a handle on my earthly desires. He was pissed that I had woken him up and also kind of skeptical about whether his slapping me was a good idea. I quoted, "Resist the devil, and he will flee from you," and that convinced him that we should do whatever was necessary to preserve my purity.

Jesse slapped me a bunch of times, but not on the face because that would have left a mark. Then I quoted, "But suffer not a woman to teach, nor to usurp authority over the man, but to be in silence," because I knew he'd give me a few more licks just for good measure, since he's going to be a husband soon and needs the practice.

Then he went back to bed because he had to get up at four in the morning to start a part-time job delivering newspapers. Megan demanded that he get a job before they get married, so Jesse hoped that it would shut her up for a while.

"Do you think we might be able to hire my brother, Jesse, as a support rep?" I asked my boss the next day. Maybe Jesse could take Cynthia's job—why not try to kill two birds with one stone?

"We're already at maximum head count for the department," she said.

"What about Cynthia? Can't we get rid of her and replace her with my brother? He's a great worker, just like me," I said.

My boss smiled. "Kyle, even though Cynthia is a temp, we treat everyone here like family. She is doing a great job.

Maybe your brother should check the available company job listings on the website."

"But Cynthia scares me," I blurted out. "I think she's out to get me." I didn't mean to let that slip, but I hadn't been sleeping well, and plus I was exhausted from touching myself a bunch of times every day.

My boss looked at me. "Kyle, have you been to see the doctor yet? Because it sounds to me like you need to make an appointment. We need you healthy." She smiled again.

"I'm trying to be healthy, but the devil . . ." I started, but then my boss said she had to go to a meeting and ushered me out. I guess I can't expect a Nonbeliever to understand what it is like to wrestle with evil.

Cynthia sat next to me in the booth at the prayer meeting that night, which meant that I had to hold her hand during the prayers. I was nervous, but I did it anyways. Cynthia has big hands, and her skin felt dry and tight. My hands were slippery from being nervous, but fortunately the prayers only lasted a few minutes. Once the pitchers of Bud Light showed up, I started feeling better.

"Isn't it awesome that He brought us together to join in His fellowship?" I said. Cynthia smiled at me and nodded. I tried to send her a subliminal message saying, *Don't even try to screw with me. I know you are a pawn of Lucifer.*

"Kyle, can I ask you a question?" Cynthia said.

"Sure. I'm an open book, especially when it comes to Him," I said.

"Are you a virgin?" she asked. I almost spit out my beer.

"Cynthia, we're all virgins in His eyes," Tim said.

I wanted to say, *Easy for you to say, Tim. You're getting blown at lunch by Gina, Miss I'm a Virgin because Fornicating with Girls Doesn't Count.*

Instead I said, "I'm committed to Him and that's what He demands."

Cynthia blinked. "Wow," she said. "That's heavy duty. Aren't you like thirty?"

"I'll be thirty-two in June," I said. "He makes it easy for me to avoid temptation until I'm married."

That wasn't exactly true, but I didn't want to let on to Cynthia that I was having a hard time staying pure. All the devil needs is for a Believer to show weakness, and he pounces.

"Don't you feel like a freak?" Cynthia said.

"I think that people who have sex before they're married are the freaks," I said.

I thought I saw Gina and Tim exchange a look.

"Okay. Good to know," she said.

Then she turned to talk to Gina. Tim was blathering on and on about the hockey scores, but my mind kept wandering back to Cynthia. Maybe she wasn't a pawn of Lucifer. Maybe she was just a nice older lady who was trying to find Him. Maybe He wants me to show her the way. After a few pitchers, it was hard to tell what He wanted me to do anymore.

"Kyle, would you mind walking me out to my car?" Cynthia said.

"Sure," I said, but I felt the hair on the back of my neck stand up. I hoped things were going to be different, but the devil was baiting me, I could feel it.

I had this feeling that I was floating outside of my body, hovering over myself, as I watched myself walk Cynthia out to the empty parking lot, trying hard to chat about work or whatever, but then she stopped and leaned against her car.

"Kyle, have you ever kissed a girl before?" she said.

"Sure," I said, "He allows kissing up to a point."

"Up to what point?" Cynthia asked.

She moved her face in close to mine and she started kissing me, and I couldn't help it, I stuck my tongue in her mouth. She stuck her tongue in my mouth, and I started to have thick, wet visions of snakes and clouds and Him and the devil, all rolled up into one. Fire licked at my toes.

I remembered one time my dad caught me watching *American Pie* on cable in the basement.

"You are filth," he said.

Then he took off his belt and bent me over his lap. It turned me on even more being exposed like that, jeans down around my ankles with my dick in my hand, squirming with anticipation. He rarely stopped until he broke skin.

I took Cynthia's big, dry hand and started stroking myself with it over my Dockers.

"Oh," she said, "oh, oh." She unzipped my pants.

"I'm not sure this is a good idea," I said.

I came back to myself a little and tried to push her away, but then she started grinding against me. Even though I didn't want it to, my cock throbbed and I heard moans escaping from my mouth. Cynthia lifted up her big skirt, and the next thing I knew, I was inside her. Cynthia started bucking like a horse and she bit down on my lip hard.

"I bet you like it rough," she panted.

The pain made me come so hard, I saw stars. I could barely breathe, and it felt like all the air had been sucked out of the atmosphere and replaced with greenish vapor. Cynthia's acrid stench was unbearable. Smoke poured out of her vagina, burning my legs. The bile rose in my throat. I knew how angry He'd be at me for a.) ejaculating my seed, and b.) having sex with a Nonbeliever. That's not good.

"You shouldn't have done that," I said, backing away from her, sweating. My pants were sticking to my leg, just like all the other evil fornicators in the world. The devil laughed from underneath the hood of a parked car at the same time Cynthia cackled, wiping her thighs off with the hem of her long prairie skirt. Her bra strap had fallen down to her elbow, but she didn't bother to pull it up. Her eyes looked crazy in the moonlight, and her painted-on eyebrows seemed to flicker. I was afraid she might strike again if I didn't make a stand.

I grabbed Cynthia wrists. "We need to pray. We need to pray right now." She tried to twist away from me, but I pulled her as hard as I could until she made a yelping sound, like the sound our dog used to make when my dad kicked him for pissing in the house. I pushed her head down into the pavement.

"Forgive us for fornicating in Duffy's parking lot!" I yelled. "Praise Him! Praise Him!" I pushed Cynthia's head down hard, and she screamed something that muffled against the gravel.

"Praise Him, you bitch!" I jerked her head up and noticed that her frozen forehead was bleeding and a large red bump was forming over her eye. So much for my dad's theory about only Believers bruising easily. She pulled away from me, her frizzy hair full of dirt. She stood up and brushed herself off.

"Just like I thought, Kyle," she said, "you're up to no good."

"You're a whore—a she-devil!" I screamed.

Cynthia laughed.

"You and me, Kyle, we're just the same. We could be twins."

Then a ring of fire surrounded Cynthia. Inside the flaming circle, she and the devil were dancing a two-step where the devil twirled her around while tipping his cowboy hat to me. Cynthia's skirt whipped up, fanning the flames. I was terrified and wanted to run, but something deep inside told me to stay. If this was the End of Days, I wanted Him to know that I was still here, facing down His enemies.

I got down on my knees, and closed my eyes.

"Forgive them, O Father, they know not what they do," I said.

I heard myself saying, "Please go away, please go away, please go away," over and over, until I heard a door slam and the screech of car tires. When I opened my eyes, the parking lot was dark and still. The green vapor and smoke seemed to have evaporated. Maybe the earth had opened up and swallowed Cynthia back into the depths where she belonged.

I kneeled there for a while, rocking back and forth.

"Please forgive me for fornicating with a Nonbeliever pretending to be a Believer," I prayed to Him.

"Please allow me to see you," I prayed harder. "I need You to show Yourself."

It seemed like hours that I stayed there, my heart beating out of my chest, waiting for Him. Then I remembered His words: "Cleanse your hands, ye sinners; and purify your hearts." I looked up and noticed the devil hanging, like a gymnast, upside down from a light pole. The devil pointed to a hard, sharp rock. I grabbed it.

"Do not forsake me," I pleaded with Him.

I brought the rock down hard upon my temple. After a few blows, I began to feel numb, as blood first trickled, then flowed into my eyes until I could no longer see. Then with a thunderous roar, He appeared in all of His majesty, in a blazing chariot made of shooting stars, more spectacular than any fireworks display. He was so beautiful! He reached down from the sky and touched my cheek.

"I'm sorry," I said. "Please don't hate me."

He smiled a dazzling display of white.

"You are my Bud," He said.

Then His golden arms beckoned. He was urging me on toward Him, toward all the beauty that is Heaven, and so again and again, I smote.

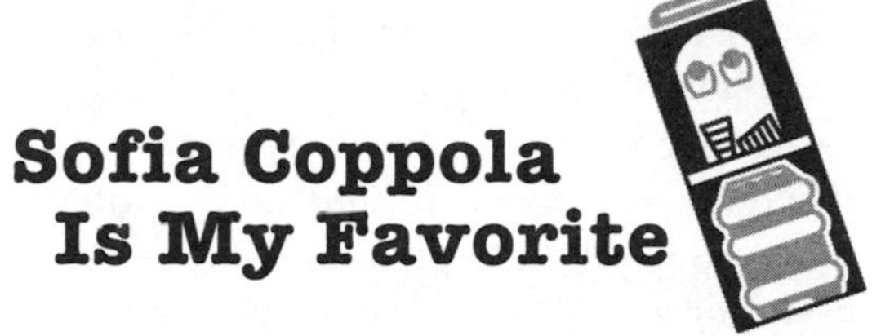

Sofia Coppola Is My Favorite

LOST IN TRANSLATION IS SERIOUSLY BRILLIANT. This guy I waited on at Hot Dog on a Stick said he thought I looked like Sofia Coppola. I had no idea who she was, so I Netflixed *Lost in Translation* and *The Godfather: Part III*, and now I am so flattered.

I really got into *Lost in Translation*—it's about this old guy trying to hook up with this hot girl, even though that would be kind of gross in real life. Maybe it worked because the girl was depressed and the old guy was charming. Also, it was cool the way that the girl smoked cigarettes in her underwear.

Most girls probably wish they were Scarlett Johansson, because she's hot and divorced from Ryan Reynolds and does ads for Louis Vuitton, but I connected more with Sofia Coppola. Sofia was an actress, but because she's so smart and hip and so not interested in being famous, she decided to become a writer-director.

I can see the resemblance between Sofia and me—I am thin, pointy-chinned like my mother, and pale except when I get embarrassed. Sofia is like me, without the Hot Dog on a Stick hat.

Sofia Coppola is the bomb.

If I were Sofia Coppola, I'd be cool and bicoastal, and I'd also own homes in European capitals and be totally intercontinental. I could afford to go out to fancy restaurants every night, although I would have a restaurant-quality kitchen in my house and be a great cook myself—

the kind of cook who creates gourmet meals by tossing together odds and ends. My fridge would be a stainless steel programmable Sub-Zero Pro 48 that keeps shit on certain shelves cooler than other shit on other shelves. My assistant would read the Sub-Zero user manual and she would program in all the right temperatures.

My assistant would not be like my sister, Carol. Carol was helping me and my mom out with the rent, but then she got all fucked up on some kind of PCP-laced brownie that her friend Phil cooked up in his daughter's Easy-Bake Oven. She ended up in court-ordered rehab for ninety days.

If I were Sofia Coppola, the kind of food I would stock in my awesome refrigerator would be ahi tuna marinated in olive oil imported from my own grove in Tuscany. I would serve it with a salad made from endive from my garden. It would feature heirloom tomatoes from the community hothouse I had built with wood taken from the reclaimed Coppola family forest in Buenos Aires.

I watched a special on the Food Network about heirloom tomatoes grown in a community hothouse, and I think I speak for Sofia when I say giving back is more precious than tons of money or fame.

I'd also make my own gluten-free bread. I would knead the dough early in the morning after yoga practice with a real yogi from Myanmar who lives rent-free in my guesthouse.

I watched a special on Nat Geo about Myanmar, which used to be called Burma. Myanmar is located in a place called Southeast Asia, which is weird because I thought Asia was its own continent and wasn't split up into different parts. Sofia Coppola set the movie *Lost in Translation* in Tokyo, which is also part of Asia, but not in Myanmar, as far as I know.

I bet Sofia knows all about geography and could name all seven continents if she had to answer that question on her GED.

Yeah.

If I were Sofia Coppola, I wouldn't have to call my friends to come by for dinner, they would just naturally show up at my house, and I would always have a fantastic spread ready. I wouldn't be stuck having to eat with my stepbrother and stepfather, Lorne.

My mother met Lorne on the Internet. He told her he was an entrepreneur, but when they decided to get married, he came clean and explained that he was on parole for robbing a CVS. My mom thought he needed a fresh start, but when he moved out here from Palm Desert, he brought along his eight-year-old son, Dwayne, whom apparently his ex had dumped him with the week before.

Sofia Coppola would never shack up with a stranger with a police record. She's way smarter than that.

If I were Sofia Coppola, I would have lots of friends. Friends who, when you call them, don't pick up and say, "I'm not home!" and then start laughing uncontrollably, until it becomes apparent that they drank a bottle of Robitussin right before you called.

Sofia's friends have enough disposable income to wear those Diane von Furstenberg wrap dresses I saw on *Project Runway*. They look great on everyone and are perfect for any occasion. If I were Sofia Coppola, my friends would be writers or directors or contestants on *The Next Food Network Star* or yogis from Myanmar, formerly known as Burma. They would not be forced to work at Hot Dog on a Stick because their sister Carol put the family finances in question due to her drug habit.

My friend Jeremy would bring along wine for dinner that cost up to $200. Jeremy is a guy I met at work. He ordered strawberry lemonade and he said that he thought I looked like Sofia Coppola, and then we started talking. He seemed like a higher-caliber person than most of the people I meet because he was carrying a shopping bag from American Eagle Outfitters, which shows that he has amazing taste.

Jeremy's dad, who is young looking and a hedge fund manager, has a wine cellar filled with thousands of wines. He lets Jeremy take any bottle he wants. Jeremy says his dad is the greatest, because he bought Jeremy and his brother hybrid SUVs when they each turned sixteen. Also, they all do volunteer work in Nicaragua together as a family during summer vacations.

Jeremy is really buff with ripped abs and a major wang, but no one knows about it because he's on the DL about it.

When I was at Jeremy's house in Agoura Hills, I admired how high the ceilings in the bedroom were. Sofia Coppola would never stand for popcorn ceilings. If she were crashing at an apartment in Paris for Fashion Week and it had popcorn ceilings, she'd stay at the Ritz instead and smoke in her underwear.

If I were Sofia, I would move out of my mom's apartment and live with some friends who have a comfy couch from Crate and Barrel that turns into a bed. If that got old, I would rent a furnished apartment above Sunset Boulevard and write my autobiography during the day and go out to the Chateau Marmont at night. Sofia doesn't ever have to live with Lorne from Palm Desert. And Dwayne too.

Yeah.

If I were Sofia, all of my friends would sit on my patio overlooking the city and sip Dubonnet on the rocks. Then Jeremy would pull out the appropriate wineglasses from the sideboard I bought from Crate and Barrel. I paid extra for the Crate and Barrel people to come over to my house and put it together for me. Then my assistant would serve us dinner—salmon, couscous, and heirloom tomato confit—and we would drink Jeremy's wine, which pairs perfectly with the meal.

Jeremy always knows what wine to bring without texting me. He and I understand each other on a higher, more intense plane. There aren't ever weird, uncomfortable silences between us.

At dinner, my friends discuss topics like interest rates and polar ice floe extinction, because we're all into current events and other intellectual shit. After dinner, I bring out a decadent, retro dessert—some kind of flaming thing like Baked Alaska that I made from scratch. I whipped it up in between yoga, bread making, picking organic veggies from the community hothouse, and working on a screenplay.

It's a screenplay that the guy who produced *Iron Man 2* has already paid me two hundred grand to write. Sofia and I have a million ideas that could all be made into awesome movies. I had one just last night when I was driving home from the mall. I thought I saw a dog in the road. It looked like a German shepherd but smaller, like a pygmy version that you might see on an Animal Planet special. I swerved to avoid the mini-dog, but then I looked back in my rearview mirror and there was nothing there.

The movie would be about this girl, played by Sofia Coppola, who works at Hot Dog on a Stick. After swerving to avoid hitting an animal in the road with her Range Rover driving home from the mall, she accidentally enters a portal into another world. The world she comes from sucks because she hates her job and her friends avoid her. Also, her stepfather is constantly offering to perform mole checks on her, and her mother unsuccessfully tries to hide the fact that she's drinking vodka, not coffee, out of her coffee mug.

The new world she enters is completely amazing, where she is a famous actress-writer-director with a rich father and a beautiful home, and she has a bunch of great friends and she knows a ton about geography.

Yeah.

So after I write that movie and get voted one of *Variety*'s "People to Watch under Forty," success will not go to my head. I will be nonchalant, even though everyone thinks I am one of the most talented people who ever walked the earth. And I'll be like, "Nah, I'm not the voice of my generation," or "Oh please, me a genius?

Now that's a hoot!" I'll use words in conversation like "hoot" and "crikey" and pepper my speech with random slang. No one will find it to be a weird affectation, like Madonna's fake English accent. Everything Sofia says seems genuine.

During dessert, Jeremy will throw me flirtatious looks, but I will be disinterested in settling down with one person. After all, Sofia and I need to experiment a lot more before we settle for banging someone more than once or maybe twice.

There will never have to be an awkward conversation between Jeremy and me where he expresses his love for me in a tedious and embarrassing way. He'll never grab his crotch and ask, "Do you want a piece of this?" He will never grope me in an obnoxious fashion. I would never have to feel guilty for flirting with him, all the while knowing that he uses way too much tongue, and not in a good way. No, Jeremy would just know that I am unattainable, so he would flirt but never go any further.

But there might be one night when Sofia and I may have had one too many glasses of Coppola Chardonnay. Maybe we gave Jeremy one too many come-hither looks over the endive. While we arranged the fresh fig and baked Camembert plate in the kitchen, Jeremy started rummaging around in the freezer, looking for ice for his Dubonnet. All of a sudden, Sofia and I found ourselves dry-humping him against the Viking range. We forgot that we left the stovetop on for the balsamic vinegar reduction, and I accidentally put my hand on the burner. I let out a yelp and Jeremy backed away. All of us looked at my hand and then Sofia noticed that Jeremy was weeping.

And Sofia and I realized, as Jeremy brushed his tears away and took the ice out of his highball glass to put on my hand, that his love would always endure. One day, when he is old and gray and living up in Nova Scotia or some other cloudy, unsettled place, he will think of me. He will wish that we could have been together forever. As he wrapped my hand in the organic cheesecloth that I keep handy for when I make my own Greek yogurt, I would wonder myself if we were somehow meant to be. But my heart yearns for freedom, and I know I won't settle down with him or with anyone else. I will want to cry, but Sofia will stop me. She says that if I allow myself to weep, I will not be the quirky, hip, brilliant person she knows and loves so very much.

And somehow, the pain of the burn on my hand will be lessened as I consider that out of all the people in the world that I might have been, I ended up becoming Sofia Coppola.

Yeah.

Then the rest of my friends will crowd into the kitchen, and everyone will be looking at my hand, saying, "Do you need to go to the burn unit?"

My assistant will rush in and take charge because that's what good assistants do.

"I know just the thing," she'll say, kissing my cheek.

She will bring out the stash of homegrown psychotropic mushrooms that I keep in a special oak drawer and put them out on one of my best Nambé platters. Then all of us will get in a single file line and feed each other the mushrooms, but it won't be freaky. Once the mushrooms take effect, the wrap dresses that my friends are wearing will start to meld together into a beautiful spiral pattern, like those Crate and Barrel placemats I've seen at the mall. We will all be united in spirit. I will reassure everyone that I am fine. I will need to finish reducing the balsamic vinegar, so I will shoo them all out of the kitchen, a mother hen clucking over her chicks. Jeremy will blow me a kiss on his way out to the patio. I will stay this way forever—young, yet wise beyond my years.

Yeah.

The *National Inquirer* will write that I am an old soul—mature, yet able to relate to youth culture, kind of like Jeremy's dad, the wine-collecting hedge fund guy. It's unfortunate, but Jeremy will eventually find out that I did it with his dad when I dropped by their house one Saturday afternoon when Jeremy was out taking the ACT. Sofia Coppola only makes it with guys who know what they are doing in that department, even if they tell her to leave as soon as they finish, and don't even offer her a glass of nice wine from their wine cellar.

When I am old, like fifty, I will still look as young and original as I do now. I will let my hair go gray, but my skin will remain unlined and my breasts uplifted, thanks to the yoga I've practiced religiously over the years. But I will still have friends over to my house every night for dinner, and we will still talk about important things, like who's their favorite on *The Next Food Network Star*.

My life experiences endow me with greater knowledge so that all those who know me, even those who only know me from my appearances on reality shows, will consider me a shaman. All men and some women will desire me. I will sleep with some of them, mostly out of curiosity, like I did with Jeremy's dad, but hopefully I won't have to sneak out of their houses with the jizz still wet on my neck.

Yeah.

I will remain curious about the world because I will constantly be tackling new and difficult projects. Maybe I'll write a screenplay about Prince Charles. Sofia Coppola wrote a movie about that French queen and did a photo shoot in *Vogue* about it. But because I bring a magical twist to everything I create, everyone will be able to identify with my characters. I can make even an old English guy into an old English guy who is majorly hot in a weird way. It's my God-given gift.

By the time I leave this earth, after my meteoric rise to fame, no one will even remember who Sofia Coppola was. But I'll remember her. I'll always remember her. She's the wind beneath my wings.

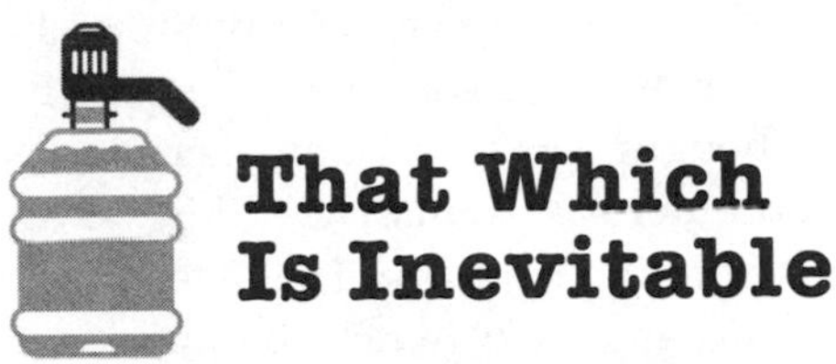

That Which Is Inevitable

DEIRDRE DEMPSEY, MANAGING DIRECTOR, STRUTS toward Joel Saunders's cubicle in a pair of strappy high-heeled sandals. She read in *Self* that high heels make a person's legs look longer. Deirdre believes long legs make the right impression.

Deirdre wears a royal-blue body-con knit top and a matching ruched skirt that purposely rides up her pale thigh. Her hair is a color called Medium Brown/Suede.

Deirdre bought her Medium Brown/Suede hair color and her body-con top and ruched skirt from Target. Deirdre finds that Target's clothing lines are inexpensive, stylish, and just plus-sized enough to fit her. Deirdre is on the lean side of the plus-sized market. This makes Deirdre feel good about herself.

Deirdre is on a mission. Earlier, when Joel passed her in the hallway on the way to her leadership meeting, she was sure he was looking at her chest and thinking, *Big ole titties.*

Deirdre hears at a higher frequency than most people, higher even than most dogs. She believes she can listen in on thoughts. Sometimes at night, Deirdre hears wailing outside her bedroom window. She hopes it is a werewolf who plans to steal her away into the brush and make her the queen of his pack.

Deirdre has huge breasts, but not so huge that she isn't able to buy bras off the rack at Target. She buys the "Sunset Minimizer" bra. It comes in a variety of colors and covers most of Deirdre's breasts. Deirdre hates hearing her breasts being referred to as "titties," even if it was just a stray thought in Joel Saunders's average mind. Employees have titties—managing directors have voluptuous, creamy breasts.

Deirdre bought a Sunset Minimizer black corset with scarlet embroidery and matching boy shorts that she plans to wear to the company Halloween party later. She is dressing up as a sexy witch. Because of her powers, Deirdre wouldn't be surprised to learn that she is related to one or several of the Salem witches.

Strutting toward Joel's cubicle, she catches the new software trainer thinking, *Deirdre Dempsey is a cocksucker*. Earlier in the week, she heard the words "viper" and "asshole" as she walked by two client services reps out on the patio, taking their state-mandated fifteen-minute breaks. Deirdre has a photographic memory.

As a managing director, Deirdre is practically everyone's boss. She believes she is fulfilling her destiny. She believes she has always been a managing director, ever since she came out of the womb, even though her promotion just came through last year.

Deirdre has an Excel spreadsheet to keep track of all the "mean employee thoughts" about her. The spreadsheet is in a folder on her computer desktop labeled "MET data."

Updating MET data can take up most of Deirdre's workday, when she isn't in meetings discussing client pain points, leadership goals, and agenda templates. If the MET data indicates that an employee has thought something disparaging about her more than three times, that employee is called into Deirdre's office and written up for something unrelated. This is about to happen to Joel Saunders. The "big ole titties" thought was his third strike.

Deirdre peeks in Joel's cubicle, which is bare and void of personal effects. Deirdre's office, by contrast, is decorated in a Zen theme. She had operations install a fountain with a smiling sun face that she purchased at Target using her company credit card. The sound of the water drowns out the employee voices thrumming in

Deirdre's ears. Joel appears to be working on a research project. He doesn't look up.

"Joel, will you please join me in my office for a moment?" Deirdre asks. She speaks in a low, affectless tone. Her inflection hardly wavers. Deirdre struts back toward her office. She can sense that Joel is following behind her, checking out her ass in her ruched skirt. Deirdre has heightened senses, like a feline. She thinks she may be a real-life Catwoman.

Deirdre closes her office door once Joel has entered. She situates herself in her chair, and makes sure that her ruched skirt is not riding high enough so that Joel could look up her skirt without trying. If Joel wants to look up her skirt, Deirdre would like him to be proactive about it. If Deirdre can prove to the CEO that 50 percent or more of her employees are displaying proactiveness, she gets an extra bonus come holiday time.

"Joel, it's been determined you have not been taking your state-mandated fifteen-minute breaks," Deirdre says in her low, affectless tone. She doesn't know or care whether Joel is taking his breaks. Deirdre often uses the state-mandated breaks as an excuse to write up employees who have thought or said mean things about her. She either writes up people for abusing the breaks or for not taking the breaks. She looks at it as a win-win situation.

Deirdre hates to admit it, but finding excuses for write-ups is getting more difficult. Her MET data spreadsheet for the year is already several pages long. Deirdre is constantly under siege, always catching wind of her employees savaging her work ethic, managerial style, and personal appearance. Deirdre has had to get very creative about write-ups. Last week, she wrote up Susi Park for changing a computer administrator password before the allotted forty-five days had passed.

According to the MET data, Susi Park thought that Deirdre had been promoted because she and the CEO were doing the Dirty Sanchez. Susi Park thought the words

"Dirty Sanchez" every time Deirdre passed near her desk. When Deirdre called Susi Park into her office, she couldn't help herself.

"Susi, what exactly is a Dirty Sanchez?" Deirdre asked.

Susi looked perplexed. "I have no idea," she said.

Deirdre asked again: "Susi, I think you know what a Dirty Sanchez is, and Susi, I need for you to explain it to me, what the Dirty Sanchez is, Susi."

Finally Susi Park broke down in tears and ultimately had to go out on stress leave.

Deirdre speaks to Joel in a direct, yet nonthreatening way. She crinkles up her face so that she appears concerned. While Joel explains that there must be some mix-up, that he always takes his breaks, Deirdre's mind wanders. She thinks about productivity strategies and quick-start guides and system setup capabilities. She suddenly remembers an old *X-Files* episode, one of the episodes early on in the initial run of the show. It seemed that Mulder and Scully might finally get together, until their mutual attraction was thwarted by Mulder's obsession over his missing sister, who he believed was abducted by aliens. When Joel finishes speaking, Deirdre modulates her voice to take on a harder edge. It is a conscious shift in tone, one that Deirdre has honed to perfection.

Deirdre says, "Joel, in the future, I'll expect you to follow the company's published processes and procedures, Joel."

Deirdre likes to repeat the employee's first name in these situations because it makes her disappointment in them appear more personal.

Deirdre is a professional. She can speak extemporaneously about many specific topics, including marketing strategies, disaster recovery protocols, product sunset timelines, and added value mapping. This is what she talks about when she and the CEO engage in the Dirty Sanchez, only in a sexier way.

Deirdre breathes deeply, inching herself into an extremely focused state. If she concentrates hard enough, she can slow her breathing down to the rate equivalent to that of an Alaskan brown bear in hibernation. On weekends for fun, Deirdre tries to bend spoons using her mind.

As she breathes, Deirdre notices a familiar emanation enter her office through the air-conditioning vent overhead. Only in a state of extreme concentration can she sense the emanation. The emanation itself is colorless and smells of cotton. Deirdre calls it "That Which Is Inevitable." Deirdre notices it circling around her office like a large but invisible bird, flying lower and lower, until it lands directly on the shoulder of her royal-blue body-con top and pecks lightly at the embroidery. Deirdre has tried on many occasions to communicate with That Which Is Inevitable, but it seems to purposely elude her. Deirdre tried to contact That Which Is Inevitable with her Ouija board one weekend, but she ended up contacting someone who spelled out that he was a friend of her great-uncle Pat's.

Joel's face has turned beet red and he stammers, reaching for a comeback. He tries to explain, this time in louder, more exacting detail, about how he can be found smoking out on the patio between 2 P.M. and 2:15 P.M., and then again, drinking a Big Gulp from 7-Eleven, between 4 P.M. and 4:15 P.M.

Deirdre relishes this type of cat-and-mouse game. She puts on a new face, one of consternation and a touch of sadness. Deirdre practices this face in front of her bathroom mirror on weekends. The face indicates that she regrets having to have this conversation, as Joel is a perfectly average employee with a clean-shaven face and a nondescript manner. But given his insubordination, Deirdre has no other choice but to punish him. Joel needs to be dealt with. He needs to be taught that managing directors do not have "titties."

"Joel, I would expect you to follow the company's published processes and procedures, Joel. HR will interoffice you the write-up notice that I expect you to sign and interoffice back to HR."

Deirdre realizes that she can see into Joel's heart, into his leached bones and overcaffeinated bloodstream. She imagines Joel's penis engorged with blood. She has a vision of Joel suckling at her full, creamy, voluptuous breasts. Deirdre wonders when she acquired X-ray vision, but is unfazed by the discovery of this phenomenon. She is reminded of another *X-Files* episode, one where Mulder discovered heretofore unexplored phenomena before getting distracted by thoughts of his missing sister.

Deirdre imagines That Which Is Inevitable is resting on her shoulder, pulling locks of her Medium Brown/ Suede hair out to the side, so that they resemble Medusa's snakes. Deirdre's thoughts wander to community forum feedback, the failure of babies to thrive, and the possible role of ancient astronauts in the creation of the statues on Easter Island. Deirdre watches the spittle form on Joel's full, thick mouth as he sputters.

As expected, Joel is finally rendered impotent. Deirdre has a vision of Joel's engorged penis deflating and sagging toward the left.

Joel leaves Deirdre's office in a huff, slamming the door behind him harder than he should. That Which Is Inevitable leaves the office behind Joel and dissipates over the call center.

Deirdre hears Joel think, *Fucking bitch*. She updates her MET data to reflect this. Then she leaves for lunch.

Lately, Deirdre has vivid dreams of being burned at the stake. She wonders if these dreams portend a day in the near future when she will spontaneously combust.

After lunch, Deirdre attends meetings, where she discusses quick-tip marketing materials and the upcoming interdepartmental company potluck and cost transaction report errors. If she concentrates hard enough, she finds that she can float effortlessly above herself. She is hoping to one day use her powers to travel through time with the werewolf who scratches and whines under her bedroom window at night.

At home after work, Deirdre readies herself for the company Halloween party. She touches up her roots with a special root wand included in the Medium Brown / Suede hair color box. She applies white powder to make her face appear otherworldly, and lines her eyes with liquid eyeliner in "blue black." Deirdre makes herself up this way on weekends before going on Skype to play board games with a group she met on Craigslist.

That Which Is Inevitable sits on the toilet seat and watches Deirdre get ready for the party. When she was young, Deirdre used to sit on the toilet seat and watch her mother get ready for parties. This was before Deirdre's mother stopped going to parties and then leaving the house altogether. At a certain point, her mother put tinfoil on all the windows to purposely shut out any sunlight.

The company Halloween party is held at Duffy's, a bar near the office. Deirdre arrives, dressed in her corset, boy shorts, fishnet stockings, a velvet cape, and strappy high heels. She passes employees dressed as zombies and vampires, and notices Joel in a toga. The DJ plays "Monster Mash." She orders a vodka tonic from the bartender, who has a plastic second head jutting out from his shoulder. She notices the bartender and his second head checking out her cleavage. The bartender hands her the change, and Deirdre puts the change in his tip jar. He smiles with his one real mouth. Deirdre gulps her drink quickly, anxious for the evening to get interesting.

Deirdre notices some of her employees staring at her. Her eardrums vibrate faster to listen in on their internal dialogue. She hears comments like *Can you believe Deirdre wore that?* and *How totally inappropriate*. Deirdre believes she looks extremely appropriate for a Halloween party. An insistent thought pervades her consciousness: it is a wish that her employees weren't such hateful assholes who hated her so much. She makes a mental note to update her MET spreadsheet, but instead drinks five vodka tonics in a row, and feels breezier than she ever does in the office. After a while, Deirdre is too tipsy to remember who thought what about her. The party is in full swing, and Deirdre wants to dance. She pushes her way onto the dance floor, out into the center, and starts to spin.

Deirdre used to spin in place for hours when she was a child. Spinning on her slippery basement floor, it felt to Deirdre as though the space-time continuum was suspended. Even as a child, Deirdre suspected that the laws of physics did not apply to her. At a certain point, she would stop spinning abruptly. Deirdre would then achieve a kind of liftoff, and for an unspecified period of time afterward, she was propelled out toward space, through the galaxies and solar systems and into the heavens. Dazzling sights flew by—shooting stars, black holes, planets being born, and suns dying in a final burst of energy. But after a while, Deirdre would always find herself back on Earth, sitting cross-legged on the concrete basement floor, inspecting the cuts and abrasions on her body, a probable result of her extraterrestrial space travel.

Deirdre's father used to joke about how he needed to build a padded room for her to play in. After Deirdre fractured her arm during one of these space outings, her mother padlocked the door of the basement.

Deirdre is spinning in place at the party, her cape whipping around her with centrifugal force, until it unties from around her neck and flies onto the dance floor. Through the din, Deirdre notices that a crowd has formed around her, standing back to give her room. Deirdre feels a pang of gratitude that her colleagues and employees have given her this freedom. She whips around, faster and faster. She hears voices as she spins—

"Look at that!"

"What the hell is she doing?"

"I knew she was crazier than a shithouse rat!"

But Deirdre is too busy spinning to care what people think. She focuses on a tiny bright light in front of her, growing brighter and larger. Deirdre's spinning intensifies. She thinks that this time, she might breach the boundaries between her and That Which Is Inevitable. A feeling of power surges within her, and she believes that she will be flung out into the stratosphere in a blaze of glory, destroying the bar and all of her coworkers in a cleansing fire. She will finally meet the time-traveling werewolf so that they can be together for eternity. But then the music stops abruptly. Deirdre feels someone grasp her shoulders to stop her from spinning. She tries to focus on the face of the person who has stopped her, but whoever they are, they have stepped away, leaving her to trip over her strappy high heels. Deirdre cannot keep her balance and falls on her behind with a hard thump. She suddenly feels dizzy and pukes down the front of her cleavage, soiling her Sunset Minimizer corset and matching boy shorts. She sits on the dance floor in a puddle of her own vomit, listening to the crowd roar. Faces contorted with laughter stream by, roiling like waves that wash over her again and again.

Then Deirdre feels a hand touch hers. The hand feels cool and smooth, as though made from a wax mold. On weekends, Deirdre makes molds of her own hands and feet with paraffin wax.

The hand pulls Deirdre gently to her feet and leads her out of the center of the room. When Deirdre looks up, she sees that it is Joel who is attached to the cool, smooth hand. His toga is stained, and his face is shiny with sweat. He finds a clean towel and helps Deirdre wipe off the vomit from her costume. He lets her touch up her own cleavage, even though her hand-eye coordination is off from spinning and she misses some of it. He gets her a glass of water from the two-headed bartender and helps her drink it. Then Joel ties Deirdre's cape around her neck. It is damp from splashed beer and scuffed with footprints. Deirdre is grateful that Joel found her cape, even though it is ruined.

"Now you're good as new," he says.

Joel pats her on the shoulder and walks away before Deirdre can utter a word. She notices That Which Is Inevitable hanging on Joel's shoulder, like a lover, whispering into his ear. She can't make out what it is saying before it disappears completely, merging into Joel's corporeal being.

Deirdre is reminded of an *X-Files* episode where the balance of sexual power shifted from Scully to Mulder, just before both of them were distracted by a mysterious object glinting in the snow.

Deirdre stumbles into the ladies' room, where two of her employees are freshening up. Deirdre cannot discern what they are saying to each other in low, hushed tones. She has no idea what they are thinking as they wash their hands and reapply their lip gloss. Deirdre tries to focus by breathing in and out, attempting to slow her heartbeat down to that of a lamprey swimming in frigid Arctic Ocean temperatures, but her mind is a blank. Deirdre fears she has heard the last of the werewolf's lovelorn cries.

As her thoughts wander to client resource management, user acceptance testing, and risk assessment, Deirdre stares in the mirror. Even in the harsh fluorescence of the bathroom, she cannot recognize herself. She has become a stranger with straggly hair, wearing a stained corset two sizes too small. She realizes that this is what it means to be earthbound. This is what it is like to be an employee.

ACKNOWLEDGMENTS

There are so many people who were integral to the creation of this book: Thank you to the faculty and my fellow students at the UC Riverside, Palm Desert MFA program, including the incomparable Tod Goldberg —your passion for teaching and writing are an inspiration. I also owe a huge debt of gratitude to Mark Haskell Smith for your boundless patience and continuing guidance.

Thank you to Corey Campbell, Cate Dicharry, Tiffany Hawk and Andee Reilly for your close reads, frank assessments and encouragement. A special thank you to Valerie Fioravanti for bringing a clearheaded and thoughtful focus to first draft chaos. Thank you to Writing Workshops L.A. for fostering an environment where writers have the freedom to forge new paths. Thank you to the journal editors who thought enough of my stories to publish them—you are the reason this collection exists.

Thank you to my agent, Gregory Messina, for your enthusiasm, calm and wisdom. Thank you to C.P. Heiser and Olivia Taylor Smith at the Unnamed Press. You both amaze me! When do you sleep? Thank you for believing in a satirical short story collection—if that isn't something short of a miracle, I don't know what is.

Thank you to my parents, who always let me make my own decisions and then didn't make me feel stupid when I made bad ones. I am very lucky to have been raised by such smart and funny people. Thank you to my sisters for all your love and support, and for never letting me forget that the middle child is the messed up one. A big thank you to my extended family and friends for all your excitement throughout this process. I am humbled and grateful for your exuberance and spirit.

And to Patrick, my best friend and the most amazing person I know.

Grateful acknowledgment is made to the editors of the magazines in which the following stories appeared, sometimes in slightly different form:

Harper's: "New Directions"

Hobart: "Gregg Fisher's Pontiac Vibe"

Inlandia: A Literary Journey: "That Which Is Inevitable"

Knee-Jerk: "Onset"

Pithead Chapel: "Winners and Losers"

The Nervous Breakdown: "Back to Me"

Zyzzyva: "Northanger Abbey"

ABOUT THE AUTHOR

Debbie Graber's fiction has appeared in *Harpers, Zyzzyva, Hobart, The Nervous Breakdown* and *Word Riot,* among other journals. She received an MFA from the University of California, Riverside.